KILLER'S DRAW

 CIRCUIT RIDER

Also By Dan Ames

The Circuit Rider
Beer Money (A Burr Ashland Mystery)
Killing the Rat
The Recruiter
The Killing League (A Wallace Mack Thriller)
Murder with Sarcastic Intent (The 2nd Mary Cooper Mystery)
Death by Sarcasm (The 1st Mary Cooper Mystery)
To Find a Mountain
Dead Wood (A John Rockne Mystery)
Bullet River (*The Garbage Collector 2*)
The Garbage Collector #1
Four (A Short Story Collection)

KILLER'S DRAW

 THE CIRCUIT RIDER

DAN AMES

THOMAS & MERCER

Published by Thomas & Mercer, Seattle

www.apub.com

ISBN-13: 9781477849033
ISBN-10: 1477849033

Cover design by Cyanotype Book Architects

Library of Congress Control Number: 2013911780

Printed in the United States of America
Originally published as a Kindle Serial, July 2013

For Elmore Leonard

draw

1: a geographical term used to describe a shallow waterway;
   a gully.

2: to remove a weapon, as in a pistol.

"Vengeance is just: Justly we rid the earth of human fiends
Who carry hell for pattern in their souls."

—*George Eliot*

EPISODE ONE

One

No one heard the shot, least of all the man on his knees, his hands bound behind him, tears streaming from underneath the blindfold. The tall prairie grass brushed against his bare chest, stuck to the tendrils of blood streaming down his belly.

The muzzle of the pistol, pressed directly into the flesh of the man's left temple, singed the skin. Then the bullet crashed through bone, brain matter, and the other side of the man's head before exiting and landing some twenty yards from the site of the execution.

It was almost as if the wind died to watch the man's death along with the killer, before gaining strength to help topple him over. He landed on his side, eyes wide open at ground level.

The shooter gazed at the dead man.

The buzzards would soon be overhead, starting their feast before any human being would make the gruesome discovery.

The location was strategically chosen, however, so the dead man would be found, and found soon.

The killer had to admit that the level of violence perpetrated upon the dead man had been severe. Great, jagged slices adorned the dead man's chest and arms. The face was battered and nearly all of the fingers and toes were broken.

The killer felt only mild satisfaction, yet a certain pride wound its way through his veil of consciousness. Not everyone could do something like this. The killing part had been easy but everything that had come before required skills and talents that very few people possessed. In fact, the killer bet that only a handful of people in the country could have pulled off what he had just done.

While the feeling was subtle, a single, coherent, starkly crystallized thought occupied the shooter's consciousness more than anything else.

The sight of the dead man in the grass created a circular argument that shuddered through the shooter's mind. Even as the killer looked at the massive amount of pain and torment inflicted upon the dead man, he kept thinking: *It wasn't enough.*

Two

"The victim was one of us," Silas said to Tower. Father Silas was head of the church in San Francisco, and hence, leader of the organization's entire Western branch. As such, he oversaw the contingent of circuit riders, one of whom was Mike Tower.

Tower set his coffee cup on the table and glanced at the older man. "What happened?"

Next to him, Bird Hitchcock splashed more whiskey into her coffee. She had provided security for Tower on his circuit ride from St. Louis to San Francisco. Along the way, she had kept Tower alive—and helped more than one man stop living.

At the table next to them, an older man in a black suit observed her liberal use of whiskey and shot her a disapproving glare. Bird winked at him, then cursed the man under her breath.

"Someone beat him, tortured him, then shot him in the head," Silas said. He drummed his fingers on the thin stack of papers before him. He shook his head.

The café area of the Grand Hotel in San Francisco was crowded as the city's business elite geared up for another day. Thin shafts of light poured down from the atrium's windows, and the smell of freshly cut flowers filled the air.

"Any idea why?" Tower asked.

"No," Silas answered. "That is why I would like you to look into it. There are . . . rumors."

"Where did it happen?" Bird asked. She drank her coffee. The thick, rich brew was balanced nicely with the burn of good whiskey. Christ, she thought, she could get used to this.

"Big River, Wyoming," Silas said.

"Don't they have a sheriff out there?" Bird asked. "Why aren't they looking into what happened?"

Silas glanced at Tower. "They do have law out there, but they don't have an idea who would have wanted to kill a man of the cloth." The older man spread his hands out on the thick linen tablecloth as if he were seeking some sort of balance. "Some of the suggestions, from what we've learned, are less than savory," he said.

Tower looked over Silas' shoulder at the entrance to the famed hotel. A couple entered, the woman wearing an expensive-looking dress, probably made of calico, followed by several porters lugging large travel trunks. It was the finest hotel in the state of California, people claimed. An odd place to be talking about a murder.

"What is it they're saying?" Tower asked. "That the preacher was doing something he shouldn't have been?"

The old man leaned back in his chair. He tilted his head back and stretched his neck, as if such a simple movement could relieve the stress.

"I don't know exactly what they're saying," he said. "I only hear rumors and theories. There are people there who believe. And they don't like what's being said about this man. The church wants to find out the truth as much as they do. And I want you to find out what really happened over there. For me. And for our fallen brother."

He slid the packet of paper across the table to Tower. "I want you to go to Big River and find out what happened." He turned to Bird. "And I want you to provide for Mr. Tower's security, a talent for which you have provided ample evidence."

Tower glanced at Bird. It had been a long ride from Missouri to California. The trip had been tough, as they had tracked down a man who had taken great pleasure in the torture and killing of women. A man named Toby Raines. Tower knew the journey had taken its toll on Bird. She had experienced the violence Raines was capable of firsthand. Still, he knew that she was the kind of woman who had no fear. As if reading his mind, Bird caught his eye, then glanced at Silas.

"Pay the same?" she asked, swallowing the last of her whiskey-laced coffee.

Tower smiled, knowing that Bird had been well compensated for her security detail. He also wondered if, on some level, she had felt the bond that had been forged between them. Tower knew that he felt it.

Silas nodded in response to her question.

Bird smiled at Tower.

"Then what the hell are we waiting for?"

Three

Bird had ridden by train before, but not like this. She had vague memories of liquor-soaked nights in the freight section. A bottle in one hand and her pistol in the other, watching the stars pass by in a blur that seemed both beautiful and ominous.

But this, this was something else.

By the time Silas had arranged for their travel, he was forced to buy the only tickets left. And those were in the forward car, first class. With an unlimited bar, all drinks were included with the ticket price. Bird was in heaven.

With their horses and gear stowed in the stock car near the rear of the train, they made their way to the luxury car. Bird opened the door and a server wearing a suit, white gloves, and a bow tie, and sporting a thin moustache, seated them at a table. Bird ordered a bottle of whiskey. Tower, a beer.

When their drinks arrived, she tipped the server. Bird figured it was the least she could do. After all, her drink was an entire bottle.

Bird poured herself a tumbler full of Tennessee mash and raised the glass to Tower. He clinked his beer mug with her glass.

"To your health," he said. The train had started, and Bird saw the slow movement of light across Tower's face. He almost looked handsome. *Almost*.

"Here's to getting to the bottom of things in Big River," Bird said. She poured herself three thick fingers of whiskey, then took a long pull directly from the bottle. It was good. Smooth, with a fine taste of smoke and lingering memories.

Tower sipped his beer and looked out the window.

Bird tossed off her whiskey and filled her glass again, then watched as Tower opened the packet of papers Silas had given them. He looked so studious she almost laughed.

"What's it say?" she asked.

Tower took a drink of beer, read a bit more, then answered.

"His name was Bertram Egans. Twenty-three years old." Tower's voice was solemn and hushed.

"Young for a preacher," Bird said.

Tower nodded.

"Looks like he was killed in the middle of nowhere," Tower said. "No rhyme or reason."

Bird's eyes traced the mahogany woodwork that trimmed the first-class car's ceiling.

"Do you think his being a preacher was the reason?" she asked.

Tower looked up from the papers. "Why is that your first question? When there appears to be no reason, why is that the initial conclusion?"

Bird noted that he had avoided her question, so she avoided his.

She shrugged off her leather overcoat as the whiskey warmed her from the inside.

Tower read some more as Bird watched an older man in the booth across from them alternatively fall asleep, wake up, then fall back asleep, his chin drooping to his chest in a predictable rhythm.

She shook her head, disapproving. First class was for people who could hold their drink.

Bird's judgment was interrupted when she heard Tower's breath intake sharply.

"What?" she asked.

Tower leaned back, his gaze fixed on the faux ceiling.

"This preacher," he said.

"What about him?"

"Says he was probably tortured. Hard to tell though. The buzzards had been at him for a while."

Four

Bird slipped the bottle of whiskey from the table into one of the long pockets in her leather overcoat, then left the first-class cabin and stepped off the train onto the good earth of Big River, Wyoming.

The smell of smoke from the train mixed with the scent of cattle, and Bird spotted the stock pens just east of the train depot. The pens were some of the biggest she'd ever seen. Not exactly miles of stockyards, but close, she thought. The cattle business was obviously alive and well in Big River.

Bird caught sight of Tower emerging from the back of the train with their horses behind him. She smiled to herself. *Gotta love a man who brings a woman her horse.*

"Where do you want to start?" she asked, taking the reins of her Appaloosa from Tower. Bird knew that because she and Tower had gone first class, their horses had gone luxury, too, being fed corn and rich grain. Bird patted her horse's flank. She already felt thicker and better fed than two days ago.

"The sheriff, I suppose," Tower said. He was looking off toward the town, a gaze of assertiveness, and, Bird thought, a curiosity about what they might find.

They mounted their horses and walked them down the main street of Big River.

The town was impressive, she had to admit. It sat astride a bend in the Bighorn River, and the land itself was a perfect plain, a smooth slope that ran down to the banks of the river.

As impressive and wide as the river was, what caught the eye of every new arrival was the impressive view of Big River and the mountains that surrounded it. It was as if someone had scraped away any hills or variations in the valley floor to create a perfect site for a town.

And it was called *Big* River for a reason. The town was booming, and its buildings reflected the river money that was pouring into the community. There was a massive schoolhouse and a solid, square building that had to be the county court-house, plus wide streets extending far beyond the main thoroughfare. Bird caught a glimpse of some of the stately homes on First Street—probably belonging to prominent merchants or some of the cattle barons who chose to reside in town.

They rode their horses through the center of town, Bird ticking off the saloons as she passed them by with satisfaction in her mind. Choosing the place to have her first drink in a new town was always her favorite part of arriving. Close second was hitting every other saloon to see if she had chosen well with her first pick.

The sheriff's office was at the south end of town, a block behind the main street. It was a square, squat building made of stone with a heavy, elaborately carved wooden door.

They tied their horses to the hitching post, then Tower opened the door and went inside. Bird followed.

A man sat behind a heavy wooden desk with a knife in one hand. In the other, he held a piece of wood that to Bird looked like a fish. As he worked the knife's edge on the center of the carving, Bird noticed a window ledge behind the man holding a neat row of at least a dozen delicately carved wooden fish.

"I'm looking for the sheriff," Tower said. Bird thought she caught a touch of sarcasm in Tower's tone, but she figured it was her imagination.

The man sighed, set the carving down on his desk, and laid the knife next to a leather blotter.

"You found him," the man said without enthusiasm, as if he were admitting to something he wasn't proud of.

"Name's Mike Tower, and this is Bird Hitchcock," Tower said. The man glanced past Tower at Bird. She knew he recognized the name. The sheriff's face was like the rest of his body— long and sad.

"How can I help you?" he asked. And then he realized he hadn't said his name, so added as an afterthought. "My name's Chesser. Sheriff Howard Chesser."

He stood, brushed wood shavings off his pant legs, and put his hands on his hips. Bird noticed he wasn't wearing a gun.

Chesser was a tall man but shaped like a pear. His shoulders seemed to cave in on his neck and the pressure had pushed his hips out to extreme measures. *Big, but soft*, Bird thought.

"I'd like to ask you a few questions about the murder of Bertram Egans," Tower said.

The sheriff visibly stiffened, opened his mouth to say something, then closed it again. He looked off to the side, then back at Tower. A few errant wood shavings fell from Chesser, as if they wanted to escape from what he was about to say.

"What is it you'd like to know?" he asked, attempting an aggressive tone that came off instead as weak and hollow.

Then, before Tower could answer, Sheriff Chesser added, "The case is currently under investigation, though. So I can't say much, if anything at all."

"Well, you answered my first question," Tower said.

"Whether the case was closed or not. So, my second question is, Do you have any suspects? Any idea who did it?"

Chesser looked down at the carving on his desk. Bird could tell he wanted to pick it up and get back to carving instead of answering Tower's questions. There was safety in the predictable.

The sheriff looked up at Bird. He seemed to be searching for something that he could be confident in and wasn't finding it in himself. "I know who you are," he said. There was a bit of smug satisfaction in his tone.

"Give that man a dollar," Bird said. "Or a wooden fish."

The sheriff plowed on. "But I don't know who you are," he said, looking at Tower. "Why are you so interested in what happened? And why should I share any details?"

Tower sighed. Bird discerned that he wasn't happy with the conversation.

"Egans was a preacher, just like me," he finally said. "Some folks with the church asked me to look into what happened out here. You're not under any legal obligation to talk to me about the killing, but I sure would appreciate it."

Bird thought Tower sounded very reasonable. Maybe just a smidgen of condescension in his voice, but only she would notice it, knowing him so well and all.

"Let me think about it," Chesser said brightly, indicating that the idea appealed to him. "Where can I find you?"

"We'll be around," Tower said. He turned and walked past Bird.

"I like your fish," Bird said.

"Thank you." Chesser seemed uncertain about the acknowledgment, but also tentatively proud.

"You can find me at the best saloon in town," Bird said. "As soon as you tell me which one that would be."

Five

The place was called Big Horn Brewery, but according to the fish-carving sheriff, in addition to its famed beer, the watering hole also had the best selection of liquor in town. A drinker's saloon, the sheriff had said. Bird liked the sound of that.

The structure itself was a large wood-frame building, freshly painted white with red trim and featuring an elaborate sign above the entrance that read BIG HORN BEER. The words had been painted with bright gold paint that Bird supposed was meant to look like beer.

Needs a second coat, she thought.

Bird opened the doors, walked inside, and immediately liked the place. It was her kind of drinking environment: all business. The main floor was a wide-open space that held nothing but tables and chairs. Along the left wall was the bar: a forty-foot-long oak slab complete with an impeccably polished brass rail. A mirror ran the same length, interrupted in sections by glass shelves filled with bottles. Beer taps were spaced sequentially down the length of the bar, each with an ivory handle.

Bird strode to the end of the bar farthest from the door and put a boot on the brass rail.

The bartender, an older man with a bald head, came over

to her. He had a huge, gray moustache with neat little twists at each end.

"What can I get you, miss?" he asked.

"A reintroduction to my two best friends. Their names are beer and whiskey," she said.

He nodded, pulled a glass mug from one of the shelves, and poured her a thick draft. With a flourish, he set it on the bar and slid it to her, the glass coming to a stop directly in front of her.

"I would have been upset if you'd spilled any," she said, hoisting the mug and tasting the beverage. The flavor was rich, with enough body to settle nicely into her stomach.

The bartender brought her a shot glass and a bottle. He pulled the cork from the bottle and filled the shot to the rim.

Bird put some money on the bar and said to the bartender, "What do you put in this stuff? It's probably the best beer I've ever had."

The man smiled, and Bird noticed his cheeks were just as pink as his bald dome.

"I'm afraid that's a trade secret, ma'am," he said. "But I can guarantee you it's the best beer this side of the Mississippi."

She drank the rest of the beer with one long pull, then slid the mug back to him. "Let me try another one, see if it's as good as the first. Call it research to see if your claim would stand up in a court of law."

"They get better with each one," he said. The beer came back at her, again sliding down the polished surface of the bar. She tossed down the shot of whiskey and easily caught the beer mug as it came to rest in front of her. She hoisted it and tasted. The bartender looked at her, waiting for her judgment.

"No complaints here," she said, licking a trace of foam from her upper lip. "Except my whiskey glass is empty and I need an answer to a question."

He filled her glass and used a towel to wipe down the already spotless bar. He had his sleeves rolled up, and Bird noted the thick forearms. This was a man who'd spent a long time on that side of the bar, and clearly took pride in his profession. Her idea of heaven was a bar like this, and her notion of a deity very much resembled a skilled server of alcoholic beverages.

"Ask away, I'll do my best to give you an answer."

Bird sipped from her whiskey glass. "Other than the sheriff, who in town might be able to tell me about what happened to that murdered preacher?"

The pink on the bartender's face and head turned nearly crimson as he looked at Bird suspiciously.

"Why would anyone know more than the sheriff?" he asked.

"Just wondering."

"We keep to ourselves here in Big River," the bartender said, his voice thin and flat. "I suggest you do the same."

He walked away from Bird.

She looked at her empty beer mug and empty shot glass. Such a sad, tragic sight. Bird silently berated herself for breaking one of her most important rules.

Never piss off a bartender.

Six

Tower closed the bible and set it on the table next to his bed. He breathed deeply, looking for the calm that always followed his reading. Today, it didn't happen for him. He stood, feeling unsettled.

At least he knew why. Silas had not given him a congregation following the conclusion of his circuit ride, which had been the original plan. Much of the reason why had to do with Bird Hitchcock, but he couldn't put all of the blame on her. The violence had followed them, and not all of it had been because of his escort's gunfighter past. Part of it was his own past, too.

And now, Silas had asked them to look into a murder. Tower crossed the room and shrugged on his black jacket. Maybe this would be his life. Maybe he had been foolish to think that a man like himself, a man who had seen more death and crime and awful things than most, could ever become a preacher.

The thought was simultaneously disappointing and oddly comforting. It was a life he knew, one he had become accustomed to over the years. A life to which many of his skills applied.

He left the hotel and started toward the saloon, and met Bird on her way out.

"Heading in for a drink?" she asked him, with a straight face but also the odd twinkle in her eye that he knew signaled she was having fun with him.

"A bit early for me, Bird," he said. She nodded. A man and woman passed them by, and they both looked at Bird with a curious expression. Tower understood why. He looked at her, the way she stood with a quiet grace, but two guns tied down, the smell of whiskey on her, and a beautiful face that oftentimes looked utterly without, maybe even incapable of, compassion. However, he knew otherwise.

"No," he continued. "I think we should ride out to the scene of Bertram Egans' murder and see what we can figure out ourselves. The sheriff doesn't seem to be in any kind of hurry to share any information with us."

She produced a bottle of whiskey and nodded to him.

"I'm ready when you are," she said.

They walked back to the hotel, mounted their horses, and headed out of town.

"So, where exactly was he killed?" Bird asked, once they'd cleared the edges of Big River. They were riding along the flat pan of the valley floor, toward the western mountains.

"Lovely little place the locals call Killer's Draw," Tower said.

"Why is it called that?" Bird asked.

Tower shrugged his shoulders. "I don't know, but we're going to need to find out," he said.

The sun was nearly touching the horizon, and the sky that had been a vivid deep blue all day long was now tinged with reds and burnt orange. Thin lines of distant clouds streaked between the tops of the mountains, fading into the background along with the last bit of glow from the sun. The tall prairie grass bent like brush strokes toward the sky's open canvas.

As they rode, Tower appreciated the vastness of the land, and wondered about Bertram Egans. What had he been doing out here? Was he traveling from town, and if so, where had he been going? If he had been going to see someone, who could it have been?

Tower also had to consider whether Egans had been killed out in this area or whether his body had been brought out to this stark but lovely valley to create distance from the murder.

The papers Silas had given him told Tower the rough location of where Egans' body had been found, but it took them nearly a half hour of riding in circles before they spotted a stake that someone had pounded into the ground with a white handkerchief tied to its tip.

Bird and Tower drew their horses to a stop and looked at the stake.

"Strange place for a preacher to be holding a sermon," Bird said. Tower realized Bird Hitchcock was thinking the same thing he was.

"Maybe he was killed somewhere else and brought here," Tower said.

"Could be," Bird acknowledged. "We need to talk to the person who found him. Or at least, what was left of him. They might have been able to tell if he'd been killed here."

Tower dismounted and walked the area around the stake. The grass was matted and clumps had been torn up, leaving mounds of dirt and exposed rocks. He saw that it was, in fact, a draw, with a thin stream of river shooting off from the main branch of the river, nearly a quarter mile away.

Tower spotted animal tracks near the center of the spot with most of the grass missing. If the murder had occurred at that spot, it had most likely rained since then because he saw no signs of blood. He glanced eastward, estimated the river was probably less than a quarter mile away, then looked back to

Bird.

She had begun walking the perimeter of the site in ever-widening circles, hoping to cut sign.

Bird stopped at her horse, retrieved from her bag the bottle she'd bought at the Big Horn, and took a swig. She corked the bottle. Tower went and stood next to her.

"Killer's Draw, huh?" she said.

Tower studied the way the draw came down from a higher meadow and cut through the valley floor. A deep gash in an otherwise faultless landscape.

He eyed the horizon and saw that the sun was now almost completely gone, the shadows from the mountains steadily racing toward them.

And that was when they heard the voice behind them. *It was thin and hollow-sounding. The word was drawn out and sounded like "bbbaaccckkkerrrrrr . . ."*

Tower turned, a little jolt of electricity raced up the back of his neck.

There was no one there.

He looked at Bird. The bottle of whiskey was gone, and a gun was in her hand.

"You heard that, too?"

She nodded.

"Sounded like someone was saying 'back here,'" she said.

Tower looked in the opposite direction, wondering if the location of the voice had been distorted by the shallow ravine. He knew sounds often echoed off water and rocks.

But there was no one there, either.

Where had the voice come from?

Bird slid the six-gun back into her holster, popped the cork from the whiskey bottle, and took another drink.

"Very strange," she said.

Tower looked up at the sky. The clouds were growing in size, and darkening.

One thing he knew with certainty.

The voice he'd heard.

It had been a woman's.

Seven

They rode back to Big River without speaking, each lost in their own thoughts. For Tower, the analysis of where Egans had been killed yielded nothing in terms of information, but the emotion the place had conveyed had been vivid and real.

He felt compassion for the young preacher, tortured and murdered in the middle of nowhere. No one should have to die like that.

Tower and Bird parted ways at the edge of town, she heading for the saloon, he going to the Elk Café for coffee.

He entered the small restaurant and sat at a table by the window. A thick woman with flaming red hair brought over a slip of paper and a coffee pot. Tower turned over his cup; she poured him a coffee and handed him the menu.

"Special today is three eggs and three strips of bacon," she said. "Don't ask me why it's a breakfast special at dinner time, I just work here." The woman smiled, and Tower immediately liked her.

Even though he had only planned to drink coffee, the smell of frying bacon and fresh bread changed his mind.

"The special sounds good to me," he said. "No harm in having breakfast for dinner, maybe I'll fool myself into doing a day's work tonight."

"It could happen," she smiled, walking back toward the kitchen.

From town, whatever storm had appeared at the edge of the mountains was nowhere to be seen. The evening looked to be clear and a little bit cold. The lights from the café illuminated the edge of the walk just a few feet into the street. Inside, there was just enough light for Tower to read.

He had brought along the papers Silas had given him back in San Francisco—the background information on Egans' murder. Back when he'd been working for the private investigation firm in Missouri after the war, it would have been called the case briefing.

Tower shook his head. He felt like he'd come full circle from that time.

Well, he thought, no one ever really knew what life was going to throw at them. It was part of what made life interesting. Sometimes, a bit too interesting.

Included in the thick sheaf was a separate batch of letters. Judging by one of the return addresses, they appeared to have been written by a woman in Boston named Evelyn Egans. After a quick scan of the first couple of letters, it seemed clear to Tower that she was Bertram's mother.

The letters were addressed to Silas and frequently referenced Bertram's application to join the church out West. Tower flipped forward and found the young man's original application at the bottom of the stack of letters.

Mrs. Egans made a solid case to Silas about why he should accept Bertram into his organization. She wrote at great length about Bertram's troubles growing up. About how his stepfather had beaten the young boy, terrible acts of violence for which his mother felt guilty. Eventually, it appeared, Mrs. Egans kicked the abusive man out of the household.

But the damage had been done.

According to the longest letter, Bertram had become violent himself. Getting into fights, committing petty crimes, and drinking alcohol. It was the last letter in which Mrs. Egans described how finally it had been the church that had saved her son. Bertram had had a spiritual revelation and his acceptance into the church as a minister was all her son wanted in life.

Tower put the letters down when his food arrived. As he ate and drank from his freshly refilled cup of coffee, he reflected on what he'd read.

It was an old investigator's technique—get to know the victim, and in doing so, ideas and theories would surface about why they had become the victim of a crime.

But Egans' story was an all-too-familiar tale. Tower had known plenty of people who sought refuge in the church due to unfortunate circumstances in their lives.

He himself was one of those people.

The stepfather angle intrigued Tower. Could it be that the man who had beaten his stepson for an extended period of time had come all the way out from Boston to finish the job? Tower had known plenty of men like that, controlling personalities who refused to let anyone ever escape their sphere of influence.

Even so, he figured it was a long shot. He made a mental note to send a telegram to Mrs. Egans and find out where Bertram's stepfather was now. If he was in jail, or dead, Tower could rule him out. But if he could determine that the man had left Boston and possibly come West, that would put him squarely in the territory of being a prime suspect.

Tower finished his meal, pushed the plate away, and declined a third cup of coffee.

While it was always a possibility that something in a victim's past was a factor in what happened, Tower had a suspicion that the crime perpetrated on young Egans had something to do with what he was doing here in town. After all, Silas had hinted about "rumors" that involved the church. It was this fact that had prompted the older man to send Tower and Bird out to Big River in the first place.

Tower paid for his meal, walked out of the café, put the case papers back into his saddlebag, and rode toward the other end of town.

According to Silas' papers, Egans had lived in a boarding-house. Tower hoped he could learn something there, and wondered idly if anyone had cleaned out the young man's room.

His investigator's instincts were coming back to him, and Tower felt a strong inclination that Egans' things were long gone.

Eight

Bird sat in the hotel's dining room, a cozy setting with a dozen tables, a fireplace, and an upright piano stationed in the corner. She imagined on busy nights, say Friday and Saturday, a gentleman could be found providing the kind of music that aids in proper digestion.

This night, only half of the tables were occupied.

The restaurant's sole waiter, a thin man with a bright white shirt and red bow tie, came to her table and popped the cork from a bottle of wine. He poured her first glass, then gave a little bow and swept away from the table.

Bird lifted her glass. Whiskey was her first love, but over the years she had gradually developed a taste for wine, thanks to an old ax thrower from a Wild West show she'd had the misfortune to take part in years back. He'd been a Frenchman and had extolled the benefits of the grape. He was dead now, shot in the head by a midget rodeo clown jealous of the burgeoning sexual relationship between the ax thrower and the show's bearded lady.

Now, Bird toasted the Frenchman's memory to the empty space across from her and drank half the wine in two swallows.

Not the best she'd ever had, not the worst, either. Supposedly, wine was good for the blood, the ax thrower had said. *Keeps the pipes clean.* Those were his exact words, as she recalled.

Bird refilled her own glass and held the stem between her fingers. She studied her fingers—long, pale, and slender. They were the only parts of her body she took very good care of, for obvious reasons. Her profession required it. Some other gunfighters she knew always wore gloves but that wasn't her style. Besides, she felt she had better control of the gun with her bare hands. A better feel.

A pair of men entered the hotel dining room, and she instantly took note of their guns. One pistol each, but the holsters were low and tied down. Not typical rigs for cowboys. They looked like gunfighters and Bird wondered if she knew them. She studied their faces but they didn't look familiar. They took a table near the fireplace, one of them with his back to the room. Probably not a professional, she figured.

Her mind wandered back to Killer's Draw. Something about that place gave her pause. Not just the weird voice she'd heard, which she was now sure had just been the wind. The wind often whistled and whined through cracks in rocks, or even through grass, making sounds that seemed distinctly human. She was sure that's what it had been. The wind.

The wine was kindling a small appetite. Bird never ate much, preferring to fill her stomach with good drink, but now she thought a small meal might do her some good. The waiter came back and she requested a steak.

When the waiter left, Bird leaned back in her chair. As usual, she had requested a table along the wall, so she could sit with her back against it.

So, when a tall man with broad shoulders and a head of thick grey hair approached, she watched him walk toward her.

The man had no gun, and his clothes were worn and slightly dirty. Bird pegged him as a ranch hand.

He stopped in front of her table. A few of the other diners glanced over at her table.

The man said, "Bird Hitchcock?"

"In the exquisite flesh," she said.

He had his right hand near the left side of his body, and he corkscrewed, swinging his arm in a wide, powerful backhand.

Bird leaned back and had just enough room between her chair and the wall so that the blow missed her entirely. She felt a waft of air on her flesh, and then the man's fingertips just barely scraped her chin on the way by.

Her gun was in her hand, pointed directly at the man's heart, by the time his arm completed its arc across his body. Before he could even bring it back, he looked directly into the muzzle of Bird's pistol.

"Inappropriate behavior for the dinner table," Bird said.

The man's face flushed red as he glared at her.

"That preacher got what he deserved," he said, his face red and the words coming out through clenched, yellow teeth. "You've got no business nosing around."

"Now how would you know what that preacher deserved?" Bird said.

"Because," the man said, and his face lost its anger, instead collapsing into a mask of sadness. "He killed my daughter."

Nine

A herd of cattle had just been brought over from their holding range outside of town, and Tower could hear the whistles and shouts of the cowboys herding them into the yards on the town's south end. Usually, herds weren't brought in this late, as the cowboys and men who ran the pens preferred daylight. It was safer that way. But cattle didn't always cooperate with the schedules of men, preferring to stick to their own chaotic timetables.

Dust from the range had spilled into town and Tower could smell the mélange of animals, sweat, and hard days on the trail.

Mrs. Wolfe's Boardinghouse was several blocks off the main street but within sight of the beautiful homes on First Street. As Tower walked, he admired the architecture of some of the big houses. He figured they must have cost a pretty penny to build. There was big money in cattle these days and the bigger the spread, the bigger the cattle baron's house.

Of course, not all of the homes belonged to ranchers. Some housed doctors, lawyers, and bankers—the moneymen who helped facilitate the town's main industry.

Tower got to the boardinghouse and studied it from the outside. It was three stories high and very wide—a big, square, utilitarian structure that nonetheless appeared well built. A porch ran the length of the building and wrapped around the side, out of sight. Three large dormers sat atop the structure, the only adornments Tower could see.

He climbed the stairs and knocked on the front door. It was stained dark, almost black, and the small brass knocker caught the dim light from the starry night sky.

After a few moments, the door was opened by a woman in a billowing green dress. She leaned the broom in her hand against the wall.

"May I help you?" she said.

"Yes, ma'am," Tower said, taking off his hat. "Are you Mrs. Wolfe?"

"I am. Good guess."

Tower smiled. "Thanks. If you have a moment, I'd like to ask you a few questions about Bertram Egans if you wouldn't mind," Tower said.

The woman's face went from open and friendly to closed and hostile.

"Who are you?" she asked.

"My name is Mike Tower. I'm a friend of Bertram's," he said. Not quite a lie, but not exactly the truth, either.

"What sort of questions?" she asked. Tower noted that the woman made no move to open the door any farther and let him inside.

"He did live here, correct? Before he was murdered?" Tower continued.

The woman folded her arms across her chest. Somewhere behind her, Tower heard the clatter of dishes as someone worked in the kitchen, probably cleaning up after the communal dinner.

"I was taught not to say anything disrespectful about the dead, so I've got nothing to say about *him*," she finally answered.

"If you would let me talk to you for just a minute or two," Tower said.

"I've got nothing to say," she repeated.

Tower was about to respond when she stepped back and quietly shut the door directly in his face.

Tower stood there, surprised by the woman's reaction.

Now what? he wondered.

Ten

Bird kept her pistol on the old man and used her boot to push the chair across from her away from the table.

"Why don't you have a seat?" she asked.

The man looked around the dining room, then sat down.

"Want a glass of wine? Will that help calm you down?" Bird asked.

"I don't want anything. I just want you to leave this whole thing alone," he said.

Before Bird could respond, someone else spoke.

"Are you that desperate for a dinner companion, Bird?" Tower asked, walking out from behind the tall old man. He looked down at the gun in Bird's hand. "I know you have sometimes have trouble finding someone to dine with, but there's got to be a better way than this."

Bird holstered her gun. She wasn't worried about the old man now that she knew why he was here.

"Actually, Mr. Try-To-Slap-A-Woman invited himself. That's what your name is, right?" she asked.

"This isn't exactly a social call," the old man said. "But my name is Hale. Ronald Hale."

Tower pulled up a third chair and sat down.

Bird grabbed the bottle of wine by the neck, took a long drink, then refilled her empty glass.

"Just so you know, Mr. Tower. Ronald here just told me that our preacher, Bertram Egans, killed his daughter."

"I'm sorry for trying to strike you," Hale said. "I just . . . haven't been myself since Dorothy disappeared. Dorothy Hale. My daughter. "

Tower glanced at Bird, then back at Hale. "So, is your daughter deceased or is she missing?"

"I know she's dead. I can feel it."

The waiter came and placed Bird's steak in front of her.

"Thank you," she said.

"Will the two gentlemen be joining you for dinner?" the waiter asked.

Tower shook his head, and Hale looked away.

"No, I don't believe they will be joining me," Bird said. "They asked me to allow them the opportunity, but I have declined."

The waiter nodded as if that made perfect sense, then retreated back to the kitchen.

"So, Mr. Hale, why are you so upset with Miss Hitchcock here?" Tower asked. "She usually waits until the evening to offend someone. Is she ahead of schedule today?"

Bird raised her glass.

"A lady always loves a compliment," she said.

Hale ignored them and said, "I understand you two are trying to clear that preacher's name, but that's a fool's errand. That man was just plain bad. I don't care if you've been hired by the church," Mr. Hale said.

"Who said we were hired by the church?" Tower asked.

"Word gets around."

"Well, you're wrong," Tower answered. "We're looking into the murder of Bertram Egans. But our only agenda is the truth."

Hale nodded.

"Well, I'll tell you the truth. That man claimed to be a preacher, but he was evil. Pure evil. He attacked my daughter, and she was never the same afterward."

"I'm sorry to hear that," Tower offered. "Tell me about the attack. How did it happen?"

Bird took a bite of her steak. It was tough and too salty but a few pieces wouldn't hurt.

"She supposedly started going to see him for advice," Hale said. "At first, the missus and I didn't think it would be a problem. It couldn't hurt, was the way we figured it."

"So, something was going on with your daughter before she started seeing Preacher Egans?" Tower asked.

"We don't know," Hale said. He glanced over toward the fireplace and seemed to see for the first time the two men who had come in earlier.

Hale suddenly got to his feet.

"I've got to go," he said.

"But I want to hear about the attack," Tower pressed. "What did Egans do to your daughter, sir?"

But by then, Hale had already begun walking away from the table.

"It sure as hell doesn't matter now," he said.

Eleven

Bird and Tower stood in the street, both digesting what the man had told them. Bird was also digesting a second bottle of wine and the few pieces of salty steak she had managed to choke down.

"So, the old man lured the preacher out of town to kill him?" Tower said.

Bird shook her head. "Not the way I see it. When he swung at me, it was like an old train pulling into the station, low on fuel. It took forever."

Tower said, "I don't see it either. There was something strange about Hale. It seemed like he had more on his mind than he was letting on."

"Maybe he doesn't really think his daughter is dead and he's wondering where she is."

Tower admitted, "Could be."

"Or maybe the girl was seeing someone else. A jealous rival who didn't like seeing his girl parading around with the new preacher in town," Bird suggested.

"Love does do strange things to people."

"Sounds like you're speaking from experience, Mr. Tower."

"I am. But who's to say it's my experience?"

He turned and set off toward the sheriff's office. Bird reluctantly followed.

"Besides, Mr. Hale was lying," Tower said.

"Are you sure about that? His swing at me felt pretty truthful. I think he wanted to hurt me."

"Maybe he did. But I think what he said about his daughter was the same type of material he shovels out of his horse's stall."

"You seem pretty sure of yourself."

"A lot of men have lied to me. Let's just say, enough for me to recognize it."

Twelve

Before they made it halfway down the street, Sheriff Chesser popped out of one of the town's three general stores. He had a plug of chewing tobacco in his hand. Bird got the feeling he'd been in the middle of a transaction when he'd seen them walking toward the sheriff's office.

"Hold up there, you two!" he called out.

"I figured he'd be sound asleep in bed by now," Bird said. "Dreaming about his wooden fish."

Tower stopped and Bird swung around him, facing the lawman two abreast. The sheriff shoved some of the tobacco into his mouth and let out a long spit. Some of it dripped onto his shirt and he wiped at it with his hand.

"I've been meaning to talk to you about that case you were asking about," Chesser said.

"You've had some time to think about it," Tower said. "I'm curious to hear your insights."

The sheriff looked at Tower and held his hands wide. "When you're dealing with all of this legal type of proceedings, you've got to move ahead cautiously. These kinds of issues can't be taken lightly."

"So, what do you have for us, sheriff?" Tower asked.

Chesser shook his head side to side. "Ain't a whole lot I can tell you about the killing of that preacher. I talked to the judge and the city attorney, they're both old friends of mine, and I guess that information is confidential. All I can tell is what's already been made public."

"Which is what?" Tower asked.

The sheriff whipped out a small piece of paper and read from it. "The body of one Bertram Egans was found near Killer's Draw. It has been ruled a murder, but there are currently no suspects in the case."

"Who found the body?" Bird asked. She shot this quick at Chesser, hoping to catch him off guard. It worked.

"Ol' Stanley Verhooven did," the sheriff said, surprising himself, along with Bird and Tower. Bird caught the faint scent of beer or whiskey on the sheriff and figured that his tongue was a bit looser than it should have been.

Realizing his mistake, Chesser looked down at the paper to see if that name had been written as "public" information. Bird guessed by his hangdog expression, that he now understood it hadn't been.

"Actually, I'm wrong about that," he said. He made a big show of taking a second look at the paper. "It doesn't say who found the body, and I don't know who did."

"Well, we're leaving town anyway, so it doesn't matter," Tower said, in a tone that was casual and offhand. Bird made a mental note to herself that when Tower wanted to lie, he was pretty damn good at it.

The sheriff perked up. "You're leaving? As in now? To-night?"

Tower nodded. "Yes, as much as we love Big River, we think it's time to move on, isn't that right, Bird?"

Bird looked at Chesser. "Hell yes, we've got to leave. That

beer place you told me about? That's the finest damn beer this side of the Mississippi. If I stay in this town much longer I'm going to drink it dry."

"From what I hear, you just might be capable of that, Miss Hitchcock, but I do hope you two make it back to Big River sometime. This here is a good town. Full of good folks."

"I believe you're correct, sheriff," Tower said. "Good night." He tipped his hat to the sheriff, and he and Bird went back to the hotel, got their horses, and rode out of town. But they didn't check out of their rooms.

"Something tells me you know where this Verhooven can be located," Bird said.

Tower said, "Sure do. We passed a sign on our way out to Killer's Draw. It had an arrow pointed east and said Verhooven Mine. Something tells me there is only one miner in the area with that name. And even if it isn't the right one, I'm sure he'll be able to tell us where to find Ol' Stanley."

Thirteen

It began to rain as they made their way out of Big River. Each passing mile brought a greater intensity to the wind and driving downpour. Bird and Tower each threw on a rain slicker, and the occasional flash of lightning revealed a valley floor overrun with newly formed raging streams.

Bird had her doubts about finding the sign to Verhooven Mine, and as the rain lashed at her face, the uncertainty only grew. They crossed a swollen streambed, struggled through thick mud, and then saw the sign.

The arrow pointed east.

When the rain abruptly ceased, Bird shook off her wet slicker and stowed it in a saddlebag. She made room for it there by taking out a whiskey bottle and raising it to her lips.

"Nothing like a drink after a rainstorm," she said. It was a long drink and the liquor warmed her, reaching out to the parts of her body that had become wet and cold. Heat from the inside out. It was the best way to warm up.

She looked at Tower. "You're wet on the outside, might as well be wet on the inside." Bird held the bottle out toward him, but he declined. Her goal was to turn Tower into a drinking companion, and she had no intention of giving up just yet.

They headed directly east, and Bird was able to discern the

slightest hint of a trail by the occasional hoofprint and stray wagon-wheel rut.

She felt the land begin to slightly rise, though the mountains were still distant. Tower filled Bird in on his unpleasant meeting at the boardinghouse where Egans had lived.

"That boy sure didn't make a lot of friends while he was here," Bird said.

"Or maybe the people he thought were friends really weren't," Tower said. "I find it strange that Sheriff Chesser had nothing to say about that. If Egans had committed some unspeakable crime, you would think the sheriff would mention it."

"Or maybe not," Bird said. "I think Chesser's head is made of the same wood as those fish he carves."

"You're probably right about that," Tower said. He lifted up in his saddle. "That must be it up there."

Bird looked down the trail and saw in the looming darkness a white tent that looked as if a blind man had built it. The posts were crooked, the structure sagging. As they approached, she could see the remnants of a cooking circle strewn about.

"Do you think the storm did this?" Tower asked, looking at the chaotic camp.

"If anything, the storm probably improved it. Only a damn fool could have put together this fiasco."

They pulled to a stop a dozen yards from the tent. Tower slid his rifle from its leather scabbard, and climbed off his horse.

"Well, miners aren't exactly known for their domestic abilities," he said.

Bird slid from her saddle, landed in mud, and drew one of her guns. She approached the tent and spotted a dozen empty whiskey jugs lined up next to the entrance.

"A man after my own heart," she said. "Those whiskey jugs

are the only things he kept organized."

Tower held his rifle across the front of his body, his left hand on the barrel, his right sliding down to the trigger guard.

"Hello!" he called out.

There was no answer, save for the sound of Bird's horse letting out a nervous whinny.

She glanced over, saw the horse's ears were pointed forward, the nostrils flaring.

"Hello!" Tower called again. "Anyone home?"

He stood, arms at his side.

"My horse smells blood, just so you know," Bird said.

"I do, too," Tower answered.

He looked back toward the trail, then at Bird.

"If you want to go in, I don't think you need an invitation," she said.

Tower took a step forward and just as he did, a thunderclap exploded above their heads, a stab of lightning lit up the area, and a gunshot followed the rolling echo. It was impossible, but Bird thought she heard the sound of a horse thundering in the opposite direction.

The lightning flash briefly lit up the interior of the tent, and Bird could see the feet of a man, swaying back and forth.

Someone was inside, hanging.

Probably by his neck.

Fourteen

Bird ducked inside the tent. She had her gun in hand, ready to shoot if someone was hiding in the corner, waiting for an ambush.

But there was no one hiding.

The tent's sole occupant, other than Bird, was a man hanging from the structure's flimsy wood frame.

He was clearly dead.

As she took in the scene before her, the smell assaulted Bird's senses: rotten meat, human despair, and the coppery scent of fresh blood.

She heard Tower enter behind her, and she spotted a lantern in the corner. Bird struck a match and lit the lantern. The scene inside was a desperate mess. Assorted mining tools were strewn about the interior, along with what looked like scrap wood and iron. A chain hung from another of the tent's flimsy wooden supports, causing it to sag inward toward the center. Another whiskey jug sat on its side, next to the shattered remnants of another.

"Did you hear a horse?" Tower asked.

"Let me check," Bird answered, stepping out the back of the tent. Immediately, she stepped away from the light thrown off by the lantern inside. She wasn't sure if someone was out here, waiting to take a shot at either her or Tower.

But had they really heard a horse? Or had it been the faint echoes of thunder?

The rain had started again, big wet drops that struck the ground with authority. Bird searched the area behind the tent, but the ground was chewed up and the layers of overlapping mud made it impossible to tell what was fresh and what wasn't. As her eyes adjusted to the darkness, Bird could make out a path leading away from the tent, toward another, smaller structure that she assumed was the mine entrance. That could wait until first light. She had no desire to explore a mine shaft in the middle of the night.

Bird walked in a wide circle around Verhooven's camp. She saw nothing that caught her eye, nothing that seemed out of place. Then again, it was night and the rain had been falling hard. Whatever tracks or subtle disturbances in the area were impossible to spot now.

She found their horses and brought them back to the front of the tent. Bird took a moment to retrieve the whiskey bottle from her saddlebag. She had briefly entertained the idea of helping herself to some of the whiskey from one of the jugs inside the tent, but those smells were too much even for her. She would use her own supply, for now.

Bird tied the horses outside the tent, then went back in where she found Tower standing, his rifle leaned up against the table in the corner. He was turned toward the dead man.

Bird went and stood next to him.

"Mr. Verhooven, I'm assuming," Tower said.

The dead man wore filthy coveralls and a stained shirt. His neck was stretched, the head tilted at an unnatural angle. His eyes bulged and his tongue protruded from his mouth.

Bird studied the dead man's face. She saw blood dripping

from the corner of the man's eyes.

"He hasn't been dead long," Bird said.

"Just a minute or two," Tower said. "That ended up being the difference between murder and suicide."

"What are you talking about?" Bird said.

"I think we really did hear someone riding away. If we hadn't, we probably would have jumped to the wrong conclusion."

Tower lifted his leg and used the toe of his boot to push the dead man. The effort caused the body to slowly twist, and reveal what had been pinned to the corpse's shirt.

It was a yellowed sheet of paper with thick black words scrawled across the front.

I killed the preacher.

Bird turned to Tower and said, "Why would—"

But before she could finish, they both heard a voice that seemed to come from a distance, yet at the same time closely surrounded them both. The effect was unsettling, and Bird felt a cold breeze along her neck.

The voice was faint, and the words weren't clear. But it was a woman's voice.

The same one they'd heard.

At Killer's Draw.

EPISODE TWO

Fifteen

For once, the blood was her own.

Bird stared at the back of her hand. She had just finished coughing, not an uncommon activity these days, she had to admit. But when she expected to maybe see a bit of spittle, instead, she saw blood. Not a lot. But even a little was more than she liked to see.

The bright-red splatter ran across her hand and dripped a little onto her wrist.

Bird grabbed the whiskey bottle from her saddlebag and helped herself, swishing the amber liquid around her mouth to rinse out the metallic taste. She wiped the blood from her hand on her horse's neck.

She straightened in the saddle and looked out over the valley in front of her. She was behind Verhooven's mine, studying the trail of the mystery rider she was sure had been involved with the miner's murder. Or suicide, as someone had probably been hoping to make it appear.

Tower waited until the morning to load the body onto the back of Verhooven's horse and head back to Big River, so Bird waited with him and then set off to find out if there really had been someone else at the mine—and to see if that someone was responsible for killing Stanley Verhooven.

A hazy sun hung overhead, the deep recesses of the valley below still shrouded in early morning fog. On the ridge to her east, Bird saw a mule deer across an open meadow, startled by something or someone. It raced across the open space and in seconds was back in the tree line, deeper into safety.

Bird nudged the Appaloosa and they moved forward. The trail had already taken them at least a mile from Verhooven's camp, but the tracks were becoming more and more difficult to find.

Of one thing Bird was sure: there was only one rider. He apparently wanted to get away from the scene as quickly as possible, but once he had, he took greater care in covering his tracks. Bird already noted how the rider had swung wide and skirted open patches of dirt on the trail, opting for sections that were covered in long grass or pine needles. Someone riding normally wouldn't do that, unless the trail was treacherous. The rain had been prodigious, but the route was fine. There was no need to veer off unless the goal was to lead followers astray.

Bird forged ahead and moved as quickly as possible, but studying the ground made the going slow. She wasn't a natural-born tracker. Bird had ridden with some genius trackers in her time; men, and one woman, who could read the ground like an open book and could interpret minute disturbances with confidence and clarity.

Bird had learned a few tricks from them, but she went more with instinct than any definite idea about whom she was following and where he might be going. It was nearly an additional quarter mile before she found another track. Just the edge of a hoof, barely noticeable along the crumbling path.

She dismounted and studied the edges of the track to decide how long ago it had been made, when she smelled smoke. At first, she thought it might be from a campfire. But as she stood and covered the butt of her gun with her hand, she changed her mind.

It was cigarette smoke.

Her horse smelled it, too, and snorted.

Bird slid the six-gun from its holster and climbed back on the Appaloosa. There was just the tickle of a breeze coming at them, so the smoker couldn't be far ahead. She moved forward slowly, walking her horse ahead with caution. She had covered a lot of ground in the last hour or so, but now was not the time to race ahead blindly.

She crested a small rise in the trail and saw a man sitting on his horse, facing Bird.

He was tall and rangy, wearing a long brown duster, with a hand-rolled cigarette dangled from the corner of his mouth.

His black cowboy hat was low over his eyes—two brilliant blue eyes peered out from underneath the rim at Bird.

The man exhaled, and a long stream of smoke immediately caught in the breeze and blew toward her.

"Took you long enough," he said.

Sixteen

Big River was just rousing itself from slumber when Tower arrived, trailing behind him a horse that carried the dead body of Stanley Verhooven.

The morning sun was bright and a shaft of light that cut across the buildings illuminated the particles of dust and dirt stirred up by the never-ending motion of cattle in the stockyards. A young boy emerged from a doorway, glanced at Tower and his unfortunate companion, and ran ahead, calling out to someone.

If memory served him correctly, the undertaker was at the end of the street, just past the courthouse and tucked discreetly around the corner.

But Tower didn't make it that far.

"Whoa, hold up there!" a voice called out.

Tower glanced over to the doorway of a law office and spotted Sheriff Chesser. Two men wearing stiff black suits and dubious expressions stood behind him. The sign above the building read THOMAS & ANDREW CONWAY, ESQUIRES.

Tower brought the horses to a stop.

"What the hell is this, preacher?" Chesser asked, as he stepped from the building's porch onto the street and walked toward Tower.

A few more people began to appear outside the storefronts and saloons, glancing toward them. Some turned and went on to finish whatever business they were transacting; others turned and walked toward them, wanting a closer look at what was appearing to be the morning's top attraction.

"I think that's up to you, ultimately, sheriff," Tower said.

"What kind of answer is that?" Chesser responded. "Are you getting smart with me?"

"Not at all, sheriff." Tower tugged on the horse's reins behind him and tossed them to Chesser. "I'm simply saying that you'll need to figure out what this is. After all, you're the highest law in this town, correct?"

The two men behind Chesser chuckled.

"Damn right I'll decide what this is. Murder is the first thing that comes to mind." He headed over to Verhooven's dead body.

"Yes, it might be murder. Or suicide. Or an accident. Or something else. But I'm sure you'll get to the bottom of it."

By now, a small crowd had assembled around the men, forming a tight circle. Sheriff Chesser leaned down to study the face of the dead man.

"That's Stanley Verhooven," he said.

"See, you're making progress on the case already, sheriff," Tower said.

Chesser glanced at him, then turned to the crowd.

"Burt and Glen. Take ol' Stanley down to the undertaker. You," he said, pointing at Tower. "You need to tell me exactly what happened and why I shouldn't arrest you right this very minute."

"Lock him up!" someone from the crowd shouted.

"Get a rope!"

Tower glanced around. There wasn't a friendly face to be found.

"Wouldn't you rather question me somewhere private, sheriff? This seems like a very public forum for me to be answering questions."

"What, you have something to hide, preacher?" Chesser asked.

"Not at all."

"So, tell us what happened."

"We—"

"Who's we?"

"Bird Hitchcock and I went out to question Mr. Verhooven regarding his discovery of the body of Bertram Egans."

A murmur spread through the crowd.

"When we got there, Mr. Verhooven was dead. He'd been strung up, and a suicide note was pinned to his clothes."

"What note?" Chesser asked. "Burt! Bring him back here!"

The men hauling away Verhooven's body stopped and led the horse back to the sheriff. Chesser cut the ropes holding the body in place, and Verhooven slid to the ground, landing on his back in the street.

The note was still attached to his shirt.

"I've got a huge problem with this, preacher," Chesser said.

"I figured you might think it was suspicious."

"It sure is. You see, Stanley Verhooven was illiterate. He couldn't write a single word to save his life."

Seventeen

"Well if it isn't Downwind Dave," Bird said.

The corner of his mouth not occupied with the cigarette was turned up in what Bird supposed was meant to be a sardonic smile.

She knew the man hated his nickname.

"And I'll be goddamned if it isn't Bird Hitchcock." His voice was low and harsh, probably from years of what was between the man's lips.

Bird recognized the tall, lanky man as David Axelrod, a gunfighter from Laredo, Texas. Bird had once worked side by side with him for the same employer—a rancher determined to bluff the town council into not enforcing the laws against him. Bird had taken a week's pay then quit. She couldn't remember what had happened between the rancher and the town, but figured it ended badly. It usually does.

"What are you doing way up here?" Bird asked. "Thought you Texas boys liked to stay close to home."

"Ah, we're just like you Bird," Axelrod said. He took one last deep drag on the cigarette, then flicked it into the middle of the trail. A thin tendril of smoke accompanied its landing. "We go where there's money and booze."

Bird laughed. Axelrod got the nickname "Downwind"

when he'd been caught with a sheep farmer's wife and was chased through a pasture by the wronged husband and his four full-grown sons. He'd gotten covered in shit, and although he'd escaped, he'd been unable to get rid of the stink for months.

"So what kind of money have you been finding up here, Dave?" Bird asked. "Are you freelancing, or working for Stanley Verhooven? As I recall, you weren't exactly the type to become a miner."

Axelrod smirked at Bird and she noticed the relaxed slump of his shoulders dissipate when her question landed.

"Oh, there's always money to be had somewhere," he said. "But hell no, I ain't no miner. Only thing I like to mine is a bottle. Just like you, Bird."

Axelrod's horse shifted impatiently and Bird noted the way the gunfighter tried to move to position the sun shining behind him over his shoulders and into Bird's eyes. But she wasn't concerned. She could see him just fine.

"You have anything to do with that old man being strung up?" Bird asked. "I've been following the trail of the bastard who did it. Not sure why I stumbled on you."

"Now why in the hell would you care about who killed some old man? Unless you was shacking up with him or something. But I figure even you could do better than that."

Axelrod cackled at his own joke.

"No, old men aren't my cup of tea. Deadbeats are my taste, which is why I was always kind of sweet on you, Dave."

Axelrod chuckled again.

"The truth is, I'm looking into the murder of a preacher over in Killer's Draw. Seems this old miner found the body. And now someone killed him. Strange, don't you think, Downwind?"

"Coincidences are a helluva lot of fun, aren't they, Bird?" Axelrod asked. He leaned forward, laughing, as he drew. It was a smooth, fluid motion, unhurried but very fast. Axelrod's gun was halfway out of its holster when Bird shot him out of his saddle. The two slugs tore into the breast pocket of his shirt and he managed to get his gun all the way out of his holster but then it slipped from his hand as he slid from the saddle, landing near his still-smoldering cigarette in the middle of the trail.

Axelrod's horse, now riderless, bolted and ran the other direction.

Bird held her gun in her hand, smoke rising from the muzzle. She looked at the dead man on the ground.

"Stupid, smelly bastard," she said.

Eighteen

"Seems a mite suspicious, preacher. I tell you about Verhooven being a witness, and you ride back into town with his body. I got half a mind to put you in jail," Chesser said.

Tower allowed himself to be squired directly into the law offices of Thomas and Andrew Conway, per Sheriff Chesser's suggestion. It was clearly a place Chesser was comfortable with, and Tower was curious. Why was the sheriff so tight with these lawyers? Clearly, they were the big law firm in Big River, with their office in a prime location and in a substantial building. But when Tower had ridden into town with Verhooven's body, Chesser had emerged from the law office's front door.

Tower was impressed with the law firm's office. The parlor was decked out with a mahogany floor, antler lamps, and a crystal chandelier. Settees lined one wall, on the other were oil paintings depicting the migration out West.

"I'm Thomas Conway," the first brother said. He held out his hand and Tower was surprised by the man's powerful grip.

"And I'm Andrew Conway," the other brother said. Tower pegged him as the younger sibling, but not by much. They were both tall and broad shouldered, with blond hair and pale blue eyes.

"Mike Tower," he said.

They were ushered into a room dominated by a long table made of rough-hewn pine.

They all took seats around the table and Tower felt as if he were going to trial, but he didn't mind—his goal was to get more information than he would give. It would be easy, especially as he didn't really have anything to hide. Also, having worked a long time ago in a very different life as an investigator, he was used to attorney's offices and the kind of conversations that typically occurred in them.

"So, how did you come to find Stanley Verhooven dead?" Chesser asked, with a quick glance toward the lawyer brothers that did not go unnoticed by Tower. It seemed the brothers were going to let Chesser lead the way and focus on observing.

Tower considered his response. He had nothing to hide, but he wasn't about to provide unnecessary detail with two lawyers in the room.

"If I killed him, why would I bring him back into town so everyone could be a witness?" Tower said, opting to ask a question rather than provide an answer. He enjoyed his own response so much, he added another question. "And exactly why would I kill him?"

Chesser looked hard at Tower, then turned to the brothers. Clearly, he had reached the limits of his interrogative abilities.

"So, are you here on official church business?" Thomas Conway asked, stepping into the prosecutor role. "Possibly doing some damage control?"

"It's pretty simple, gentlemen, and I don't know how much more plainly I can put it. I would simply like to know who killed Bertram Egans and why," Tower said. "Nothing more, nothing less."

"But if you could prove that the crime had nothing to do

with the church, well, your supervisors back in San Francisco wouldn't mind that all, now would they?" the other brother said.

Chesser nodded enthusiastically. He liked where the brothers were taking this.

"Everyone loves the truth except those working to obscure it," Tower said. "I just want to find out the truth."

Chesser pulled a small piece of wood out of his pocket, and began rubbing his thumb over it, sizing it up as his next project, Tower figured. He idly wondered if the sheriff set out to carve an image he already had in his mind, or if he let the block of wood provide the suggestion.

"I sure don't know about all these questions you're asking, Mr. Tower," Chesser said. "I just have to look at the facts. And the fact is, I told you about ol' Stanley, you rode out there and came back with him dead. Seems like a pretty obvious case of cause and effect to me."

Tower almost laughed at the sheriff's smug satisfaction with his own line of questioning. Instead, he ignored him.

"What do you two know about the murder of Egans?" Tower asked the attorneys. The younger brother looked out the window toward the street. The older one, Thomas, looked directly at Tower. Tower could tell he didn't like being questioned himself.

"Didn't surprise me at all someone killed that preacher," he said. "Some of the nastiest, dirtiest, most women-hating men I've ever met in my life have been preachers."

The block of wood being turned in Chesser's hand came to an abrupt halt. The younger brother turned to Tower to see his reaction.

"Yes sir," Tower said. "We're almost as bad as lawyers."

Nineteen

It took Bird nearly a half hour to track down Axelrod's horse and coax it into letting her grab its reins. The sound of gunfire and the sight of blood were apparently new to the animal, which was mildly surprising to Bird. Her Appaloosa was a seasoned veteran at this point.

Bird brought the horse, a big roan, back to the rise in the trail where its previous owner had waited for Bird. Axelrod was still face down in the dirt, the pool of blood now black.

A tree just off the trail made a temporary hitching post as Bird tied the horse to its solid trunk. She then hoisted Axelrod's body onto the back of the horse, tied his hands and feet to the stirrups, mounted the Appaloosa, and turned back toward Big River.

As she rode, morning turned into early afternoon, with the sun at its peak and creeping toward the start of its descent. The wind died down and the dust from the trail hung in the air.

Bird drank from Axelrod's whiskey bottle as she rode, retracing her steps back toward Verhooven's place. There was no one else on the trail, and as she rode, she wondered what Mike Tower was doing back in Big River.

She had to grudgingly admit that they made a good team. Bird was good with guns; Tower was better with people. For the kind of work Silas had outlined for them, hell, maybe they could actually accomplish something. She even figured they just might be able to find out what happened to Bertram Egans.

It became hotter, and as Bird crested a rise, she realized she was at the edge of Killer's Draw. The trail sloped off to the west, but Bird guided the horses to the edge of the water and made a picket with a fallen branch and a good length of rope.

As the horses walked to the water's edge to drink, Bird slipped Axelrod's saddlebags from his horse and slung them over her shoulder. She also reached into Axelrod's pockets.

"Don't mean to pick your pockets, Dave, but who knows what I might find?" She dug out some papers and a box of matches, then carried everything over to a tree that was casting a wide shadow on the grass beneath it.

She sat on the soft grass, leaned her back against the tree trunk, and took a drink from the whiskey bottle. It was quiet here, and the breeze that was nonexistent back on the trail now moved with a cool forcefulness that dried the sweat on Bird's forehead.

Bird set the bottle down next to her and opened Axelrod's saddlebags.

There was not much there that interested her. Aside from another unopened bottle of whiskey, which she would put to good use when she moved on. Bird glanced over at the bottle next to her. She'd kill the rest of that with another drink or two.

The rest of Axelrod's gear was expected—a bedroll, some food, and ammunition for both a rifle and a pistol.

Bird set the saddlebags aside and looked at the papers she'd fished from Axelrod's pockets.

There were two pieces of paper. The smaller one turned out to be a receipt from the general store in Big River for the food and ammunition. The other slip of paper was a short note, with a hand-drawn map that Bird instantly recognized as the rough directions from Big River to Verhooven's mine.

The note was short and sweet:

This is where you'll find him. $200 and whatever you can take. Meet back in Big River in a week.

-P

Bird folded the note and map, then put both of them into her pocket.

Who the hell was "P"?

Twenty

Big River, Wyoming, was not a small town. Tower had known that the minute he and Bird stepped off the train. The cattle yards alone sprawled for miles outside the city limits and business was booming.

He left the Conway brothers' law office and now walked along the street. A town this size was interesting to Mike Tower. Small enough so that most people knew each other; big enough to merit hierarchies of power within the community.

Since his arrival in Big River, Tower had seen, and heard about, a place called the Big River Club. From what little he had gathered, Tower surmised it was a place where Big River's rich and powerful congregated to clue each other in on land deals and political maneuvering.

And now, his stomach was telling him it was time for a good meal, and although the Big River Club's prices would probably put a dent in his meal budget, it might be worth it. He was getting nowhere with regular townsfolk regarding the Egans murder. Maybe some of the denizens of the club would be more forthcoming.

Tower had glimpsed the club from afar, but seeing it up close, he couldn't help but be impressed. It was a two-story structure that occupied at least half of the block it sat upon.

A huge porch wrapped around the perimeter of the building, with ornate posts that led up to a shingled overhang.

He counted at least seven chimneys, a dozen or so gables, and a half-dozen men lazing on the front porch, smoking cigars and generally gazing out at Big River with expressions that conveyed a mix of confidence and proprietorship.

Tower climbed the wide front stairs and went inside. The lighting was dim, and a thick layer of cigar smoke wafted across the great room, despite a slight breeze from the open windows on each side.

The inside of the Big River Club was just as impressive as the outside. Turkish rugs were spread evenly throughout the main space, covering beautiful mahogany floors with intricate mosaic borders. The space itself was subdivided into a dining area complete with dozens of tables and chairs made with a rich, dark wood. Several groups of men were already seated, all of them at various stages of eating and drinking. Delicate glass vases filled with fresh wildflowers sat atop each table.

A hallway branched off from the dining room with doors that Tower figured led to private dining spaces.

A bar ran along the opposite side of the great room with a large mirror behind it and glass chandeliers spaced every ten feet or so down its length. Oil paintings and frescoes covered the walls. A few men stood at the bar—one of them studied Tower with great interest.

Tower made his way toward the dining area. A man emerged through swinging doors at the rear of the dining room. He wore a stiffly starched black suit, had tousled, bright red hair, and a fixed smile.

"How may I help you, sir?" the man asked.

"I was hoping to get a bite to eat," Tower said.

"Have you ever been to the Big River Club?" the man asked.

"First time."

Tower caught the look of uncertainty on the man's face, and wondered if dining was reserved for members only. He preempted any objections by saying, "Sheriff Chesser recommended I give this place a try."

It seemed to work. The man gave a little bow and gestured for Tower to follow him to a table near one of the large windows. It was a table for two, so Tower took the opposite chair, which afforded him a view of the club's front door.

Bird Hitchcock had rubbed off on him.

A waiter appeared with a menu.

Tower glanced at the selections, then played it safe by ordering roast beef and mashed potatoes. He turned down the suggestion of wine or brandy.

Bird hadn't rubbed off on him *that* much.

His food came quickly and he devoured it. The flavors and quality of the food were exceptional, worth every penny of the substantial cost.

Tower then accepted an after-dinner cigar from the maître d'. He got it going and was enjoying the smoke when the man from the bar who had studied him upon his arrival approached his table. He had on a white shirt, pinstripe pants, and a matching pinstripe vest. He also wore spectacles and carried a bag on his shoulder. His youthful, freshly scrubbed face brimmed with enthusiasm, despite the fact that Tower estimated him to be middle-aged.

"Excuse me, sir, but are you the preacher who brought in the body of Stanley Verhooven?" the man asked. His voice was precise and crisp.

Tower looked around the room. The diners at the other

tables were focused on their food or each other, and the men at the bar were busy ordering drinks from the bartender. No one seemed to be paying them any attention.

"Who wants to know?" Tower replied.

The man smiled. "My name is Roger Jeffire. I'm the editor of the *Big River Bugle*, as well as its lead reporter."

Jeffire pulled out a notebook and thick black pencil.

Tower sighed.

"May I ask what your name is?" Jeffire asked, his pencil poised.

"Look, Mr. Jeffire," Tower said. "I appreciate your interest, but nothing I've done is newsworthy. I found that dead man and brought him to the sheriff. End of story."

"Are you sure that's all there is?" Jeffire asked, with the kind of tone that told Tower he knew there was more to it.

"Quite sure," Tower said. He looked at his cigar.

"And it's got nothing to do with the young preacher who was murdered out in Killer's Draw?"

"I have no idea," Tower said. "Do you?"

The reporter didn't answer, just studied Tower with a strange intensity.

"In any event," Tower said to fill the silence, "I figure Sheriff Chesser will get to the bottom of that."

Jeffire snorted in derision.

The red-haired maître d' appeared out of nowhere and asked Tower, "How was everything tonight, sir?" He shot at a glance at the newspaperman.

Jeffire ignored the man.

Tower paid his bill and got to his feet.

"It was excellent. And I think now I will enjoy my cigar out of doors."

He nodded to his host and brushed past the reporter, who followed him.

Tower walked down the stairs and into the street.

"One more thing," Jeffire said.

Tower turned and stared at the man. Several men were now on the porch, looking directly at Tower and the reporter.

"What?" Tower asked.

"I know why Bertram Egans was murdered."

Twenty-One

Bird felt at peace, in the shade of the tree near the draw, and continued to drink the dead man's whiskey. She felt the gauzy cloud of drunkenness coalesce into something denser and more blanketing, then let her shoulders relax as the alcohol's comfort slowly settled upon her.

There had been times when she was younger that she regretted drinking, and the questionable behavior that sometimes followed. Those days were long gone. But now, as she did occasionally, Bird thought back to her first drink.

She was maybe ten years old, living with a family of farmers who couldn't grow a plant if they lived in the jungle. The crops were miserable, the husband was a drunk, the wife bitter, and the kids just trying to survive.

The husband had taken to chasing after Bird. The last time, he'd been drunk and Bird had just finished building the fire in the stove. He'd come up behind her and lifted her dress. Without a moment's hesitation, she'd turned around and jabbed him in the face with the hot end of the poker. He was so drunk, the heated iron made it all the way through his cheek into his mouth before the pain registered. And then he began to scream.

He swore he was going to kill her, so she barricaded herself in the pantry where she'd found one of the sonofabitch's whiskey bottles. Without hesitation, she uncorked the jug and took a drink. And then another. And another. Immediately, she'd felt at peace as the warmth enveloped her. From that day on she knew it was her escape.

Of course, being a little girl, the alcohol immediately caused her to pass out. When she awoke the next morning, feeling dizzy and disoriented, one of the other children whispered through the door that the farmer had gone into town to see the doctor. So, Bird walked out of the pantry, stole a horse, and rode away, taking the whiskey bottle with her.

Drinking had quickly become second nature to Bird. And now, sitting in the shade, watching a horse drink with a dead man over his back, she understood her perspective had matured even more. It was simply a part of life. Bird recognized and accepted that she and booze would always share the trail.

Bird coughed then, and followed it with another, deeper cough that tore her lungs and sent a fine spray of blood from her mouth.

She ignored it.

The Appaloosa trotted toward her and Bird got to her feet. A few clouds had rolled in, momentarily blocking the sun, and the wind felt cool on her face. Bird grabbed the horse's reins, freed the animal from the picket she'd created, and was about to do the same with Axelrod's horse when a blur of color and motion appeared in the periphery of her vision. She drew her gun and looked in the area where *something* had been. She was sure of it. But now, she saw nothing. Bird questioned if it had merely been some type of reflection from the water and the rocks in the stream.

Then she saw another hint of movement just inside the long grass on the opposite side of Killer's Draw.

Bird quickly climbed into the saddle and steered the Appaloosa toward the grass. In the air above her, she could hear something soft and faint. A high tone too thin to be a voice.

Her horse shifted its feet and flared its nostrils.

The sound died away quickly, but not before Bird was convinced.

She could be wrong, she told herself. After all, nearly the entire contents of a bottle of cheap whiskey was now inside her, and the sun was back out from behind the clouds, bearing down relentlessly.

But for a moment, she knew what she'd heard.

It was a voice.

And it belonged to a little girl.

Twenty-Two

"We're being watched," Jeffire said, glancing over Tower's shoulder to the Big River Club's wraparound porch. "Someone is always watching around here."

"Where can we talk?" Tower asked.

"Come by the newspaper office after dark, tonight. I'll tell you what I know. In the meantime, have you talked to Walter Morrison?"

Tower shook his head. "No. Who is he?"

"He's the church secretary."

The papers Silas had given him said nothing about a church secretary named Walter Morrison. If he'd known there even *was* an employee of the church, he would have started there.

"Have him tell you what he knows; it will be good background for when we chat tonight." Jeffire tipped his hat. "Until then."

He began to turn and walk away but Tower stopped him.

"Does it have something to do with the disappearance of Ronald Hale's daughter?"

Jeffire gave Tower a curious smile. "No. Probably because Ronald Hale doesn't have a daughter. He lives alone."

Seeing no response coming from Tower, Jeffire departed, whistling as he went.

What is it with this town? Tower thought. He hadn't seen this many liars since his last card game on a Mississippi riverboat near New Orleans.

He sighed, felt eyes staring at his back, and at first stifled an urge to look behind him to see who had an interest in the conversation. He then turned, as if to relight his cigar, and spotted two men on the club's porch. They were opposites. One was small and thin, dressed like an Eastern dandy, while the other one was huge, easily six inches taller than Tower and much wider. The little man had a foot raised and resting on the porch's railing. The bigger man just stared at Tower.

Tower blew smoke into the air and smiled at them. The little man nodded. The big man clenched and unclenched his ham-sized hands. Tower thought he heard a knuckle crack.

He turned his back on the men. He had no idea who they were, but made a mental note to eventually put names to the faces.

He walked down a side street and made his way to the church. The structure, although substantial, still somehow conveyed an impression of humility. Maybe it was the simple flower beds around the front steps or the unadorned sign telling parishioners the schedule of services.

Tower finished his cigar, dropped it into the dirt and ground it down with his boot heel, then climbed the stairs and went inside the church.

Two sets of benches twenty deep ran from the front of the church to the back. They were made of simple pine, stained dark with use. Off to one side was a row of candles. The other side held a few tables with stacks of papers and several dog-eared bibles.

Near the front of the church were two confessional booths—both doors were open.

The altar was on a slightly raised platform, and was relatively ornate for such a simple room. It was made of a blond wood, with hand carving on the legs and front edge of the altar's top.

The ceiling above the altar was painted a unique grayish-blue that Tower had never seen before and the borders of the ceiling and the wall where they met were inlaid with a delicate gold finish.

In Tower's estimation, it was a beautiful church.

A door at the rear of the altar opened and a man stepped out. Tower instantly assessed him as one of those people you would never remember; one who would blend into a crowd completely.

He was of average height and average build, had light hair, and wore dark clothing.

"I thought I heard someone come in."

Tower nodded and walked toward him.

"You're Walter Morrison?" he asked.

The man looked at Tower more closely.

"I am," he said. "And you're the preacher I've heard about?"

"That would be me."

Morrison stepped aside, and gestured toward the open door behind the altar.

"Come in, we've got a lot to talk about."

Twenty-Three

The top of the grass brushed against the chest of the Appaloosa as Bird nudged the horse forward. It seemed like a crazy idea. What would a girl be doing out here alone? There were no ranches or farms nearby. There was nothing but a broad, flat valley until you got to Big River.

So had she really seen someone?

Bird wondered if there was something strange in Axelrod's whiskey. Maybe it was one of those newfangled concoctions made with strange pharmaceuticals. Bird had heard some interesting stories about creative chemists back East and the crazy things people did when they ingested their creations.

She pulled the bottle out and looked again at the label. No, just straight whiskey. And the bottle had been unopened; she'd broken the seal herself.

A firm wind was blowing down the length of the draw. Small rocks moved beneath the horse's hooves. A bird flew high overhead, its shadow briefly moving across Bird's path.

She rose slightly in her stirrups and looked out over the top of the grass. It was especially thick here, probably because part of the stream branched off and provided extra irrigation to the ground nearest the stream. Where the grass extended, it slowly declined in height as it radiated out from the streambed, forming a gentle slope, barely perceptible from a distance.

Bird studied the ground but saw nothing that seemed unusual in its presence. She saw no clues, no tracks of any kind, animal or human.

"Hello?" Bird shouted. Her voice echoed across the valley in waves.

There was no response.

She sank back into her saddle, pulled out the bottle of whiskey and drank. It was nearly empty.

Bird waited.

Another bird flew overhead.

And then someone laughed behind her.

Bird twisted in the saddle, bringing her gun out with the motion. She brought the Appaloosa around with a start.

There was no one behind her.

Bird felt a moment of confusion that instantly morphed into anger. She did not enjoy being toyed with.

Bird dug her heels into the Appaloosa's sides and charged ahead, back to the riverbed.

No one was there.

Bird again studied the ground, walking her horse in tight but expanding circles. There were no tracks other than her own.

And then Bird realized something else.

Downwind Dave and his horse were gone.

She rode over to where she'd left the pair, but there was no sign of them. Bird scanned the surroundings.

"Goddamn, this is really starting to annoy me," Bird said.

There would have been no reason for the horse to run off. There was water and plenty of grass. Plus, Bird had glanced over less than a minute ago and seen the horse right there. Now, there was nothing, just the tracks from where they'd come in, but no sign of the horse leaving. Bird kept studying the ground until she spotted something at the edge of the stream.

It was faint, and probably nothing, but it caught Bird's eye.

She dismounted the Appaloosa and studied the small indentation not more than two inches from the water's edge. Bird looked into the water, at the smooth stones and small pebbles that lined the bed of the river. Their general color and sediment was uniform. She reached in and turned one over, noting the darker and rougher rock bottom.

No one had walked through the stream recently. If they had, some of the stones would certainly have been turned over.

Bird looked back at the mark, and realized it was really two small marks.

Both seemed to hint at an edge of some sort. If it was the mark of a boot, it would have to be a very small boot. Much too tiny to be a man's.

Which meant it was a woman's.

Or a child's.

Twenty-Four

"Father Silas sent you out here?" the man asked.

"He did," Tower said. He stuck out his hand. "Mike Tower."

Morrison shook Tower's hand and said, "You're a circuit rider? Is that what I heard?"

"I am . . . or was. It depends, I guess, on what Silas has in store for me. Right now, he wanted me to come out and see if I could shed some light on what happened to Egans. Seems like he wasn't getting enough answers from the sheriff."

Morrison frowned. They sat at a rickety wooden table on equally rickety chairs. An unlit candle sat on the center of the table. A lopsided bookshelf was the only other item in the room. The shelf was crammed with small books bound in leather, all of them well-worn.

Tower looked at Morrison. Closer up, Tower could see he was much older than he first guessed. Late sixties, maybe even early seventies.

"Chesser doesn't like to share information, or really do much of anything," Morrison said. "Never has, never will. I'm not surprised Silas was frustrated. I've tried to find out what I can, but I'm an old man. No one's got much to say to me, especially knowing how I feel . . . felt . . . about young Bertram."

"And how did you feel about Egans?" Tower asked.

"I liked him, of course!" the old man practically barked at Tower. "He was a great kid. Wanted to help. Cared about people. He was a fine young man. Don't let these mealymouthed yokels tell you any different."

"Oh, they've been telling me a much different story than you are, that's for certain. They all seem to think that whoever killed him deserves a giant thank-you. Maybe even a street named after him, the way they talk."

"They're full of manure."

"Why do you say that?"

"Because they don't know what they're talking about. Bertram had big ideas for this town, and for this church. He was very curious about what made people tick. Why they made certain choices in their lives. He was a very passionate young man. I admired him. When he was engaged, he was very passionate."

"What do you mean by 'when he was engaged'?"

Morrison shrugged.

"I guess I'm referring to the times he seemed like he had something else on his mind. Like he had a secret. He would never tell me about it, though. Even if I did ask, which was only once or twice."

Tower thought about that.

"You think highly of him. No one in town apparently feels that way. So, who do you think killed him?"

Morrison's shoulders slumped. "I have no idea."

"What do you know about Ronald Hale? He tried to tell me that Egans killed his daughter, but then I heard that he doesn't have a daughter. In fact, no kids at all, not even married. Why would he lie about that?"

The old wooden chair creaked as Morrison got to his feet. "I have no idea why Mr. Hale would say such a thing. Don't know the man, to be honest. But it sounds to me like someone knows why you're here and is maybe trying to confuse the issue."

"That occurred to me," Tower said.

Morrison put his hands on his hips. "If you don't mind my asking, why did you become a preacher, Mr. Tower?"

He'd been asked that before, but still, Tower paused before speaking. "I think because I spent a good amount of my life hurting people. And at some point, I wanted to help them instead."

"I thought about becoming a man of the cloth, too," Morrison said. "But I just never felt the calling. I think a lot of men choose the profession, or the profession chooses them, for the same reason you just described to me."

Morrison put his hand on the back of his chair and leaned forward.

"I think that was the case with Mr. Egans. That feeling I had that sometimes his mind was somewhere else? I think he *was* somewhere else. I think he was in the past. *His* past."

Tower thought back to the letters he'd read from Egans' mother. The hints at a troubled past.

"I think you are probably right, Mr. Morrison."

"And if I am, I think there's a good chance that whoever wanted him dead knew something about his past, too."

Twenty-Five

The town of Big River appeared between her horse's ears, and Bird felt a mixture of relief and unsettledness. It felt like a long time ago that she had ridden out to Verhooven's mine with Tower.

Now, she trotted her horse back to the hotel, flipped a couple bits at the hotel manager, and asked for beer and whiskey to be sent to her room, along with hot water for a bath. Once she'd dropped her gear off, the beer and whiskey arrived first, so she filled a mug with beer, then dropped a couple shots of whiskey into it, sat on the edge of the bed, and waited for the hot water. It arrived several minutes later, and her tub was filled. She shucked her clothes, hung her gun belt next to the tub, grabbed the beer and whiskey, and slid into the soapy hot water.

It felt wonderful.

Bird sank into the water and rinsed her face. She reached out for the mug with a fresh serving of beer and whiskey, then sunk far enough into the water that the scar on her chest wasn't visible.

She closed her eyes, pictured the odd images back at Killer's Draw. The voice seemed so clear. If it was the voice of a child, where had the child gone? And was that the print?

Bird glanced down and saw the scar on her chest now

peeking out just above the waterline. It had been carved there years ago by a man known as Toby Raines. A man who was now dead, thanks to the gun hanging within inches of her hand.

It was a violent country. Almost everyone she had ever known had either killed someone or knew someone close to them who had been killed. She had a feeling things would change eventually. Already, it seemed more law and order was visible, especially now that the railroad had made its full circuit across the country.

Bird drank again.

She wondered what she would do. How long would she ride around with Tower? It still seemed odd to her. A woman like her—bottle in one hand, gun in the other. Piles of dead men behind her. And now she was working side by side with a preacher?

She didn't believe in God.

But she sure as hell believed that life enjoyed making every day a mystery.

• • •

The knock at the door came after Bird had gotten out of the tub and changed into clean clothes.

"Who is it?" she asked. The gun was already in her hand before the words left her mouth.

"Lynching party," Tower said.

Bird rolled her eyes.

"Come in," she said.

Tower opened the door and came into the room. He looked at Bird and she saw him hesitate. There was a chair next to the washbasin so he pulled it out and sat on it.

"Want some beer or whiskey?" Bird asked.

Tower looked. "Beer, please." She poured a glass and handed it to him.

"So, you go first," he said. "What did you find out?"

"Well, I found out who killed Verhooven. A man named Downwind Dave Axelrod."

"Never heard of him."

"You won't be hearing anything from him now, either."

Tower looked carefully around the room, as if she'd stashed the body under the bed.

"No, he's not here. I lost his body at Killer's Draw, but that's another story," Bird said. "What about you?"

Tower set aside his curiosity, filled her in on his meeting with the reporter, and Morrison.

"Sounds like the Big River Club is my kind of place," she said. She put her head back on the pillow and stretched out on the bed. She felt very tired all of a sudden. Probably the combination of a bath and a boatload of whiskey.

"Probably not, the bar was pretty small," Tower said.

"Was there a bartender?"

"Yes."

"Then it'll do."

"So, it sounds like Axelrod was hired by someone to kill Verhooven," Tower said, after Bird explained the discovery of the note and what it said.

"That's how it was signed?" he asked. "With just a P?"

Bird nodded.

"Plenty of people in town with a P in their name," Tower said.

"Yeah," Bird said. "But how many with enough money to hire their very own gunfighter?"

Twenty-Six

They walked into the hotel lobby and Tower immediately spotted the two men who'd been watching him from the porch of the Big River Club.

They sat at a table facing the stairs, the little one with a cup of coffee in his hand. The big one sat in what looked like a dollhouse chair beneath his immense bulk.

Since they were situated facing the stairs, Tower figured they were now keeping a more direct eye on them, so he approached the table.

"May I help you gentlemen?" Tower asked.

The big man lifted his head and looked at Tower, his eyes peering with apparent boredom from beneath heavy eyebrows. The little man smiled, put down his coffee cup, and traced a pattern on the tabletop with his index finger.

"Now why would you be asking if we need help? Do we appear to be in need of assistance?" the man asked. His voice was high and chirpy. Tower thought he sounded like a ten-year-old boy.

"I'm a man of the cloth, sir. I'm always looking to help people," Tower answered.

Tower sensed Bird behind him, moving away to the side.

"No, there is nothing you can do to help us, Mr. Tower," the man said. "I am simply enjoying a cup of this fine hotel coffee. And Carl is busy . . . being Carl." The big man displayed no apparent recognition that he had been mentioned. He continued to look at Tower with tired indifference.

"Since you already know my name," Tower said. "I'd like to introduce you to my associate—"

Before he could finish the sentence, the little man said. "Bird Hitchcock. Pleased to make your acquaintance."

Tower looked at Bird, caught the look of annoyance on her face. He turned back to the little man.

"And you would be . . ." Tower said.

"Name's Benjamin Hackett," the little man said. "And this is my associate, Carl Weller."

"I already mentioned that I'm a preacher. Do you mind me asking what you do for an occupation?"

The little man chuckled. Tower noted the bright blue eyes, the way they seemed to stare at him with none of the emotion carried by the rest of the man's face.

"I am an entrepreneur, Mr. Tower. I create my own opportunities."

"What kind of opportunity are you creating now?" Tower asked.

"Too early to tell."

A brief silence hung between them. Hackett continued to trace a pattern on the tabletop with his index finger. Weller continued to glower. Tower decided that nothing important would be gained by continuing the conversation.

"Well, good luck, gentlemen, I'm sure we'll be seeing you around town," Tower said.

"That is very likely," Hackett said.

Tower and Bird left the hotel.

"What the hell was that all about?" Bird asked.

Tower explained how the two men had watched his discussion with Roger Jeffire and how he felt they'd staked out the hotel to keep an eye on them.

"I'll be damned," Bird said. "Well, I've got some news for you, Mr. Tower. That little man's name sure as hell isn't Benjamin Hackett. Or maybe it is, but that's not what he called himself down in Laredo. There, he was known as Henry Jones. A helluva card cheat and quick with a gun. Carries one up his sleeve and another one in his boot."

"I figured he wasn't being completely honest with me," Tower said.

"And that big man, he was known as Mr. Seven. Probably because he's almost seven feet tall. He likes to beat men to death with his bare hands. I never saw him do it, but I saw the body of one of his sparring partners. Pretty gruesome."

They made their way to the newspaper office as Tower thought about the two men.

"Why would they be so interested in us?" he asked.

"No clue. But I'm not done yet. Do you remember when Ronald Hale confronted me at the restaurant about Egans and his daughter?"

"His fictitious daughter, you mean," Tower said.

"Right. Well, just before he confronted me, two men had walked into the dining room and sat well away from me. Something about those two rang a bell, though, and I've been trying to piece together who they were, but now that I've had the pleasure of seeing Mr. Seven and Henry Jones again, it hit me."

"Who are they?"

"The two men in the restaurant were part of Henry Jones' gang back in Texas. They'd been brought in to settle a range war by making one of the warring party's members disappear. I originally was part of that group, until I realized they wanted us to simply murder everyone in cold blood."

"So, now we're facing four people at least who seem to have a vested interest in what we're doing."

"Yes, four. There were five. "

Tower looked at her and Bird nodded.

"Downwind Dave was a part of that group, too."

Twenty-Seven

The *Big River Bugle* was closed for the day. The door was shut and locked, and Bird saw no lights on inside.

"You sure he said tonight?" she asked Tower.

"He was pretty clear."

"Let's check the back."

They walked through the alley and found the newspaper office's back door. Bird tried the handle. It was unlocked.

"What do you think?" Bird asked. She looked around the rear of the alley. Across the way was a lumberyard and a barn. Both appeared to be locked up for the night.

She turned and saw Tower peering through a dusty window into the dark interior of the office.

"He did tell me to meet him here," he said. "So, if we went in, technically, we have an invitation. We wouldn't really be breaking the law."

"Yeah, I'm sure Chesser would cut us a break," she said.

Tower shrugged.

"Well, I've made myself welcome with a lot less of an invitation than that," Bird said. She pulled the door all the way open and went inside.

The room smelled of oil and metal. She found a lamp on the desk nearest the door and lit it.

A faint light was cast throughout the room, enough to see that she and Mike Tower were the only people in the office.

"Maybe you upset him somehow and he's not going to show," Bird said to Tower. "You probably said something that was highly insensitive and you offended him. You have a knack for doing that."

"Unlikely," Tower said. "I think you're confusing me with you."

Bird continued walking through the office. There were four large tables laid out with papers, rulers, pens, and razor blades. Bottles of ink and stacks of books were scattered on every available surface.

"Sure looks like a newspaper office," Bird said. "Must not be much news going on after dark."

"That's when most of the news happens," Tower said. "Maybe everyone's out covering the shadowy life of Big River."

"Maybe," Bird said. "Or maybe they're home having dinner."

Bird stopped and looked at a desk that was set farthest from the door, away from all of the other tables. "What did this man say to you, again?" Bird asked.

"He said he knew why Egans was killed. But he didn't want to tell me right then because your pals back at the hotel were listening."

"What do you think—"

They heard galloping hoofbeats come to a stop behind the office. They walked out to find a young boy sitting astride a big bay horse. Both the horse and the boy were out of breath.

"I'm looking for Mr. Jeffire," the boy said.

"So are we," Bird answered.

"Is something wrong?" Tower asked. "Looks like you were riding somewhere in a hurry."

"Hell yes something's wrong!" the boy exclaimed.

"What is it?" Bird asked.

"I can only tell Mr. Jeffire," the boy said, regaining his composure. "He and I have an arrangement. I bring him what I hear, and if it's worth it, he pays me. This is going to be worth a lot."

"How much?" Bird asked. She pulled a wad of bills out of her pocket, peeled off a few, and held them up for the boy to see.

"That'll do," the boy said. He slid off the horse and snatched the money from Bird's hand.

"They found Mrs. Parker," he said. "She's dead."

"Where?" Tower asked.

"Killer's Draw."

Twenty-Eight

Bird knew the way by heart at this point. So, despite the dark of the night, only a few stars overhead and a half-moon shedding a thin veil of light on the terrain, she was able to push the Appaloosa as fast as she could.

She couldn't help but wonder if the boot print, or shoe print, or whatever the hell kind of print it was, was that of the woman the boy said had been found killed. Bird also wondered about her own tracks, and if she'd left any sign of her stop at Killer's Draw. It wouldn't look good if they could tie her to the same spot where a woman had been murdered, especially if only a matter of hours separated them.

Bird slowed her horse to a canter and covered the ground a bit more carefully as the smooth plain gave way to more loose rocks. Soon they saw the glow of a fire and some makeshift torches that produced enough light to make visible the watery gash that was Killer's Draw.

They slowed their horses to a walk as they approached.

Bird spotted Sheriff Chesser with a handful of men from town. They were all heavily armed with both pistols and rifles, looking as if they would like nothing more than for a target to ride up and present itself.

On that very thought, Bird and Tower came to a stop and the sheriff approached them.

"Whoa, hold up, what are you people doing out here?" he asked. "Seems like every time there's a murder you two are close by."

"We heard you had another murder on your hands, sheriff," Tower said. "Same place as Bertram Egans. Figured the two killings might be related."

"I think that's a pretty big assumption, preacher," Chesser said. "I'd advise you to stay clear of this area until we're done."

Bird and Tower left their horses east of the draw, and walked toward the crowd of men standing around two dark shapes on the ground.

"Don't touch anything, you two," Chesser said to them, as he retreated back to the group surrounding the bodies. Bird noted that he didn't go to the front of the group, but assumed a position in the middle, as if he were just another one of the crowd.

Bird wove her way until she could get to the front of the group.

The body closest to her was that of a woman killed with an extreme amount of violence. There were deep slashes in her body and great chunks of flesh were ripped from her. Her dress, what was left of it, lay in a heap next to the body. Her legs were spread. And stuffed into the space between her legs was a giant river rock.

Next to her, Bird heard Tower take a deep breath.

Bird knelt down and studied the woman's feet. She had one shoe on and Bird immediately knew it was too big to be the one that left the track she'd seen earlier.

Tower moved down to examine the next body, and Bird followed.

This one she recognized.

Downwind Dave Axelrod.

There was a knife in his hand. Both the knife and Axelrod's hand, along with the front of his clothes, were covered in blood. Bird could tell the blood wasn't from the two gunshot wounds that she'd personally delivered directly to his heart.

Tower looked at her.

Bird glanced behind them, saw that no one was listening.

"Believe me, when I kill a man, he's killed," she whispered.

Tower surveyed the distance between Axelrod and the woman, then looked back at the dark water gushing through Killer's Draw.

"If it's possible to hate a place," he said, "this is the place."

EPISODE THREE

Twenty-Nine

It started just after dawn. Tower, always an early riser, was up and had walked the town, going over what he knew so far about the murder of Bertram Egans. Now, he leaned on the top rail of a cattle fence, one of thousands at the Big River cattle yards, watching some of the longhorns being herded into the nearest enclosure. The scene was oddly quiet. It seemed that both the cowboys and the animals were too tired from the long drive to make much noise.

"Preacher," a voice behind him said.

Tower turned and looked into the faces of two men who clearly had been up all night drinking, and most likely, discussing the murder of Mrs. Victoria Parker, whose body had just been found in Killer's Draw.

"What can I do for you, gentlemen?" Tower asked. He stood casually, hands at his side, measuring up the pair that stood before him. They were about the same height, but one was a little thicker in the chest and a couple years older. Neither looked like a cowboy just in from the trail, which told Tower they were probably locals. Their clothes were clean, though, and they wore gun belts. Tower figured they just might be ranch hands working for Mr. Parker.

He could also tell by the set of the older man's jaw that he would be the first to act. And Tower knew these boys were here to act, not talk. Maybe he could change that, though.

The second one just stared at Tower, but there wasn't as much hostility in his face; he seemed the drunker of the two.

"You can tell us why you think running around and acting like a damned preacher is going to fool this whole town," the older man said. "You think we're stupid or something? Think we don't know you killed Stanley Verhooven and Mrs. Parker?"

"I haven't killed anyone," Tower said. "I can tell you boys have been hitting the bottle pretty hard. Why don't you let me buy you a cup of coffee and we can talk about your suspicions?"

The younger one turned and looked at his drinking companion.

Tower took a step closer to the men.

"I'll even buy you a nice, hearty breakfast," Tower said. "You'll sleep like babies all day."

The younger one's face registered surprise at Tower's ease. The older man appeared to grow angrier, frustrated with the lack of fear in his quarry's response.

"The hell with your cup of coffee, and the hell with your goddamned breakfast you phony damned liar," the older man said. His face was flushed red from both anger and alcohol. They both closed in on Tower until they were just a few feet apart.

"Perhaps an early lunch, then?" Tower asked.

The man's face went one degree more crimson and then his hand flashed to his gun. Tower covered the distance between them before the pistol could clear leather and he chopped down on the man's gun hand, then threw a short right hook that landed with bone-jarring accuracy on the drunkard's jaw.

The man's knees buckled and he dropped to the ground as Tower grabbed his gun from the holster and turned to the younger accuser, who jumped back, away from Tower. His hand hovered over the butt of his pistol.

"Pulling that gun out would be a very bad idea," Tower said. "Ask your boss here."

Tower now had the gun in hand pointed casually, but directly, toward the young man's chest. "You'll be dead before your iron even sees the light of day."

Tower watched the young man hesitate, then move his hand away from the gun.

Tower lowered the pistol. "Why don't you take him back to wherever he belongs, and next time he gets a great idea like this? Let him do it alone. You've got no desire, or aptitude, for this kind of thing."

The young man nodded.

Tower emptied the cartridges from the unconscious man's pistol, pocketed them, and dropped the empty pistol onto the man's chest. He looked at the younger one, who now had the chance to shoot Tower if he was so inclined.

Tower walked past him, back into Big River.

Thirty

Bird left the hotel, walked over to the livery, and got her Appaloosa and Tower's horse. She saddled them up, then brought them back to the hotel where she had agreed to meet Tower before they tried to figure out what the hell was going on in this town. Bird would never call herself the most compassionate human being to ever walk the earth, but one thing she believed in with all her heart was vengeance. In fact, sometimes she thought most of her life had been spent avenging herself, and occasionally, someone else. Not that Bird had met him, but the idea of that young preacher executed at Killer's Draw didn't sit well with her. Bird had never met Mrs. Parker either, but in the West, women were generally considered off-limits to this type of violence. She herself was the exception. But if the same person who killed Bertram Egans had also killed an innocent woman, Bird would make sure he paid the appropriate price.

She mounted the Appaloosa, felt some pain in her midsection, and started coughing. Blood spurted from her mouth and landed in the dirt next to her horse. She felt a little light-headed and she steadied herself by holding the pommel of her saddle. After a few moments, the feeling left as quickly as it came.

"Goddamn," she said.

Bird pulled out one pistol, opened the gate, and spun the

cylinder, confirming it was fully loaded. She repeated the same procedure with her left gun, holstered it, took out her Winchester and fed shells into the magazine, then slid it back into its scabbard.

She was fully loaded.

"Where the hell is that damn preacher?" she said to her horse. The Appaloosa perked her ears and looked at Bird out of the corner of her eye, then shifted her feet as if to say she too was ready to go.

"Probably off trying to help someone, the fool," Bird said. She looked at the Appaloosa. "I know that's what you were about to say."

Bird got tired of waiting and walked the horse up the street, toward the cattle pens where Tower said he was going.

Two men were walking back from that direction. More accurately, one was walking while propping up the other. At first, Bird thought the one staggering was probably drunk, but as she passed by them, she saw the man's swollen face. *Maybe he was drunk and ended up on the losing side of a fistfight,* she thought.

"Get some sleep boys," Bird said as she passed them. "I'm speaking from experience."

Bird turned the corner and spotted Tower walking with his horse in the opposite direction.

She put her fingers in her mouth and let out a long whistle.

Tower turned and began to walk back to her.

Her lungs caught after she whistled, and Bird coughed again, twice. A fine mist of blood shot from her mouth and landed on the back of her hands. She wiped them off on her pants and spit another gob of blood into the dirt. Bird nudged her horse forward so Tower wouldn't see the blood on the ground.

She wiped her mouth with the back of her hand.

All of this blood and coughing was trying to tell her something.

And she knew what it was.

For her own good, her own health, she had to make a change.

She had to stop drinking so much coffee.

Thirty-One

"Did you have something to do with that gentleman sporting a freshly busted-up face?" Bird asked.

Tower glanced up at her. She seemed especially pale this morning, her delicate face looking even more fragile than usual.

"We had a brief discussion," he said. "Let's go see if we can find out what the sheriff may have learned, or more realistically, how much he doesn't know, about what happened to Mrs. Parker out at Killer's Draw."

Tower mounted his horse and they rode to the sheriff's office, which was empty, but they saw at least a dozen horses tied up outside the Big River Club across the street. They stood side by side, hitched to the post, switching their tails at industrious flies already starting their workday.

Bird and Tower stopped outside the club and tried to see inside the windows. But all they saw were the backs of a substantial group of men that appeared to be standing around a large, centrally located table in the main room.

"Looks like some serious discussion is going on in there," Bird said.

"Sure does," Tower said.

"Want to join them? Rile things up a bit?"

Tower pondered the idea. "Probably quite a discussion going on about Mrs. Parker and your pal Axelrod."

He shifted in his saddle. They were alone in the street but he spoke quietly.

"Let me talk out loud for a minute," he said.

"The floor is yours, Mr. Tower."

"So, Bertram Egans comes to town, to take over the parish of Big River. We know from the letters that he had a troubled childhood, and that his life has taken on new meaning. His church secretary says the young man is a fine, upstanding citizen. The rest of the town, however, claims he was the devil himself. One man even claims that Egans practically killed his daughter."

Tower paused.

"Then, someone kills him. Brutally. Which usually means it's personal. However, I can't possibly think of a motive because no one will admit why, according to them, Egans was such a horrible person."

"In my experience," Bird said. "The only reason someone won't openly discuss something like that is when it's cause for great shame and embarrassment on their part. So, whatever they feel Egans did, it's something they, too, feel ashamed of."

Tower thought back to his time working for the detective agency after the war.

"In your opinion, was the handwritten note you found on Axelrod most likely penned by a man?" he asked.

"It sure looked that way. Then again, anyone can write in block letters, if it was a woman trying to look like a man."

She raised an eyebrow, thinking back to the letter she found in Axelrod's pocket, signed simply "P."

"Are you thinking the P stood for Parker? As in Mrs. Parker?"

Tower shrugged his shoulders. "The thought crossed my mind. Let's entertain the notion that whoever killed Bertram Egans also killed Verhooven. Which would mean that Verhooven was most likely murdered because of what he either saw or did around the time he came upon Egans' body. Because if he had some kind of information, he could testify about it in a court of law and perhaps name names or provide clues as to the killer's identity."

"Logical," Bird said.

"And now, we've got the man who killed Verhooven—Axelrod—dead. And on his body, a note ostensibly from the person who hired him to kill Verhooven, signed with a P. His body is found next to a woman whose last name starts with a P."

"Where are you going with this?" Bird asked.

"The big question in my mind is what is the connection between Bertram Egans and Mrs. Parker? It would be too big of an anomaly if she was completely unconnected, other than the location of both crimes."

Bird pulled a whiskey bottle from her saddlebag and took a drink. She gestured toward Tower with the bottle. "Unless Verhooven was killed for some other reason. The guy was a hermit miner. The perfect kind of person to rob. And we know that I killed Axelrod, not whoever may or may not have hired him to do anything, which also makes the pairing of the two dead bodies all the stranger."

Tower shook his head.

"Know what else I find mighty peculiar?" he asked.

"What's that?"

"How come there's no search party? No posse? No mad scramble to look for the killers? The bodies were brought into town in the middle of the night." He lifted his chin toward the

Big River Club. "And now they're in there, talking away. It's almost like they know the killer isn't out there."

"They think he's right here in Big River," Bird said.

"It would appear that way."

"You know what?" he asked. "I think you had the right idea. Let's go in there and see what kind of trouble we can get ourselves into."

"Let's hope the bar is open," Bird said.

Thirty-Two

A thick haze of cigar smoke filled the great room of the Big River Club. Tower also caught the strong smell of coffee and liquor, as well as that of the men who'd been up all night consuming both.

A majority of heads turned upon their entrance. Bird broke off and strode toward the bar where the bartender was plying his trade.

Tower headed straight for the knot of men surrounding an expansive round table. He counted six men seated in a semicircle, all dressed as if they were at an important business meeting. The rest of the group was assembled before them, as if they were awaiting instructions.

Tower instantly recognized two of the six seated men as the Conway brothers, the attorneys who'd questioned him along with Sheriff Chesser. The man seated in the middle was a huge figure, nearly as wide as two full-grown men. Tower figured he weighed at least four hundred pounds, all of which strained against his dark gray suit, and spilled out of the top of his shirt collar. He had enormous, thick hands and a square head. His complexion was a shade of red, as if his heart was overworked just pumping blood through the giant expanse that was his body.

Tower noticed the older Conway brother register his appearance. He nodded toward someone in the group, and soon Chesser, as well as Bird's old friends from the hotel, Henry Jones and Mr. Seven, stood before him.

"This is a private meeting," the little one, Jones, said. "Reserved only for members of the club. Do you belong to the club, Mr. Tower?"

"No, I don't," Tower said. "Do you?"

Jones chuckled. "I am very much a member of this club, as is my associate here."

"So the club has no standards, is that what you're saying?" Tower asked. He smiled up at the big man. Behind them, Tower noticed that everyone had stopped talking in order to listen to the exchange.

"You!" a voice boomed from behind them.

The crowd parted as the huge man from the table was now standing.

"Bring him up here," he said.

The crowd parted even more, opening up a direct path from Tower to the big circular table.

Tower approached the corpulent man.

"How dare you barge in here and try to cause trouble," he growled. His voice was as thick and bloated as his body. "I just lost my wife, for God's sake!"

"I apologize, sir, I had no intention of—"

"You certainly did! Now I could have you tarred and feathered and run out of here like a dog. You, and your whore over there at the bar."

All heads turned toward Bird. She raised her beer mug to the group.

"Good morning, gents!" she said with a big smile. "Cheers!"

The group turned back toward the man whom Tower now understood to be Joseph Parker.

"Get them both out of here," Parker said. "And you," he pointed a finger the size of a sausage at Tower. "If you stick your nose in this town's business again, it'll be the last thing you do. Are we clear?"

Silence hung over the room.

"What are all of you trying to hide?" Tower asked.

The crowd erupted, and Tower allowed himself to be pushed across the room and out the front door. Bird followed him out, still holding her beer.

"Dammit," she said. "I forgot to ask if I could join."

Thirty-Three

"Well, I was going to try to have a talk with Mr. Parker, but it appears that he wouldn't be very open to that," Tower said.

"Yeah, he's still in mourning, obviously," Bird responded. She had walked out of the Big River Club with her mug of beer, and now drank from it as they sat on their horses in the street.

"Something's been bothering me," Tower said.

"They probably sell ointment for that at the general store."

Bird finished her beer and threw her mug back toward the Big River Club. It landed at the base of the front steps and shattered into pieces. Someone peeked their head out of the front door of the club, then went back inside deeming it not worthy of closer investigation.

"If Ronald Hale doesn't have a daughter," Tower continued, "why did he make up the story and take a swing at you? Seems to me, there could be only one reason: someone put him up to it. And if that's the case, why don't we track him down and confront him? Maybe we can get him to cough up a name."

"We've got to find that damn reporter, too," Bird said. "Where the hell did he go?"

"This town has a way of making people disappear," Tower said. "They should have named it Big Mystery instead of Big River."

They rode back to the center of town, asked around about Ronald Hale, and finally got directions to his house. When they arrived at the ramshackle little building on the outskirts of town, a spotted dog barked at them from a safe distance away.

Tower knocked on the door.

It opened quickly and a small, wizened man peered out at them. His face was drawn and pinched with eyes that were probably once a brilliant blue but now were dim and red rimmed. Though he was dressed tidily, Bird noticed the man's clothes were filthy and that the house emitted a strange smell.

"We're looking for Ronald Hale," Tower said.

"What do you want?" the man practically shouted at them. He turned his head and cupped his ear with a gnarled hand.

"We want Ronald Hale, do you know where he is?" Tower said in a louder voice.

"This some kind of joke?" The man looked from Tower to Bird, his eyes lingering on Bird. He licked his lips.

"No, it's not a joke, sir," Tower said. "Do you know where he is?"

The old man cackled.

"I'm Ronald Hale for golly's sake!" he said. "What the hell do you want? I'm a busy man!"

Tower looked over at Bird.

"Is there more than one Ronald Hale in this town?" Tower asked.

"Of course not, you damned fool!" the man said. "I've lived here all my life and everyone knows me. And they all know I'm one of a kind!"

"Our mistake," Tower said. "I apologize for the intrusion."

Hale stepped back and slammed the door shut. The dog started barking at them again.

Thirty-Four

Since their pursuit of the so-called Ronald Hale who had confronted Bird had hit a dead end, they decided to focus their efforts on Roger Jeffire. They quickly learned that not only did the newspaperman live in town but he was also married.

Tower didn't know why he was so surprised to find out that Roger Jeffire had a wife. Maybe it was the man's intensity during their initial meeting at the club, or Tower's own impression that the man was married to his newspaper, or simply the fact that he hadn't mentioned a wife in their short conversation.

Regardless, they learned that the Jeffires lived on Third Street, just a few blocks from the *Big River Bugle* office.

They knocked on the door, which was immediately opened by a woman in her fifties, with gray hair pulled back into a tight bun and an anxious expression on her face.

"Oh," was all she said.

Tower knew from her reaction that Jeffire was still missing. "My name is Tower and this is Bird Hitchcock," he said. "We were hoping to have a word with Mr. Jeffire."

The woman stepped back and held the door open for them.

"You may as well come inside. I was hoping to have a word with him, too."

She led them to a sitting area off of the kitchen. The simple room held a wooden table with four chairs, though it was oddly dominated by a bookshelf that ran the length of the room.

The woman saw Tower studying the books. "It's Roger's collection," she said. "He always says that you can't spend too much money on books." She shook her head. "My name's Martha, by the way. Can I get you something to drink? Some coffee? I have a fresh pot."

"No thank you, ma'am," Tower said.

"I'll take some coffee and if you've got a little something to add some kick to it, that would be great," Bird said.

"I believe we do have something like that," Martha Jeffire said. "I've been known to enjoy a tipple now and then, as well."

She went to the kitchen.

Tower turned to Bird and whispered. "Why do I get the feeling that she's looking for her husband, too?"

Bird shrugged her shoulders as Martha Jeffire returned.

"Here we go," she said, armed with three cups of coffee on a tray.

"I brought you a cup even though said you didn't want one," she said to Tower. "I don't want you feeling left out."

"Thank you," Tower said, accepting his cup, noting the delicate white porcelain with its light blue pattern. He thought it looked like an Oriental design.

"It's from China," she said, again seeming to read Tower's thoughts. "Not sure which dynasty, but I love Chinese porcelain. It's probably good we live out here in Big River, and not back east or in San Francisco. I'd burn through our money faster than Roger could make it."

"Do you know where Roger is?" Tower asked. "He was supposed to meet us last night at the paper's office, but he was nowhere to be found."

Martha Jeffire shook her head. "When he gets something between his teeth, he's unstoppable. Doesn't matter how many people he's agreed to meet at a certain time. So don't feel bad. He must have gotten wind of something and took off after it. He's like a mad dog that way. Stories come first, people second." Her voice took on a heavy quality and Tower wondered if she was including herself in that statement.

"Probably the sign of a good newspaperman," Tower said.

"Any idea what story he might have gotten wind of?" Bird asked. "There was a pretty big one last night out at Killer's Draw."

"I heard about that. Mrs. Parker, right?"

"That's what they're saying," Tower said.

Martha Jeffire shook her head. "Never met her, but I'd heard good things about her. When will all this killing stop?"

Tower tried the coffee. It was excellent and he was glad Martha had brought him a cup. "Did Roger say anything the last time you saw him, or give any indication of where he might be headed?"

Martha Jeffire leaned back her chair and folded her arms across her chest. "Before I met and fell in love with my little bulldog reporter, I was going to be a lawyer. Instead, I developed a hobby. I would try to judge the character of people I just met. Funny thing was, the more I practiced, the better I got. And I can tell you from over thirty years' experience, you two seem like good folks."

She turned to Bird. "You seem a little on the wild side, but in a good way."

"That might be the nicest thing anyone's ever said to me, ma'am," Bird answered.

"So, I'm going to be honest with you, even though Roger

would probably not be happy with me. He doesn't like to give any information out about a story before he's had a chance to publish it."

She poured herself another cup of coffee, went into the kitchen, and added a shot of whiskey to it, and did the same to Bird's.

"Roger went over to Harlan's Crossing, about a half day's ride north of here."

"Do you know why?"

Martha Jeffire nodded.

"He wanted to talk to your dead preacher's girlfriend."

Thirty-Five

"Let's talk about this at the saloon," Bird said. She led Tower over to the Silver Bucket Saloon and took a seat at a table in the corner with her back to the wall. This was the kind of saloon she spent the most time in—a nothing-fancy kind of place with only one kind of whiskey for sale: cheap.

Tower got a bottle of whiskey and a glass from the bartender, brought it to the table, and put it in front of Bird.

"This one's on me," he said.

"Just one glass?" Bird asked. "I thought I was making some progress turning you into a hell-raiser."

"No, I can't keep up with you, Bird." He took a seat and leaned back, stretching his legs out. "I'm not even sure you can keep up with you."

"What the hell's that supposed to mean?" she asked, splashing whiskey into her glass.

"You look kind of pale," Tower said. His eyes were steady, and Bird momentarily felt unnerved by the compassion she saw. "Are you all right?"

"Jesus Christ, when did you turn into my nanny?" she asked. "I'm just fine, thank you very much."

Tower held his hands up. "Just thought I'd ask." He looked around the saloon, then back at Bird. "For some reason, I think Roger Jeffire may have been headed in the right direction."

"I've heard plenty of stories about preachers and some more-than-willing ladies." Bird said. "I believe they refer to it as tending to the flock?"

"Most preachers are human, too, Bird," Tower said.

"A man of the cloth is still of the flesh, right?" she asked. She drank the whiskey, felt its raw burn in her throat. She felt the need to cough but swallowed it, not wanting to spray blood in front of Tower.

"I don't say that because I have any theories on Bertram Egans," he said. "It's more that I was impressed with Jeffire. If he felt there was enough evidence to pursue this lead, then there must have been more to it."

"No one said anything about Egans having a girlfriend, and Mrs. Jeffire didn't know even know her name," Bird said. She tossed down her whiskey and refilled her glass. "Then again, they haven't really said anything about him except how happy they are he's dead."

"I'm skeptical he had a girlfriend. But there was some reason Jeffire went over there."

"So, why aren't we on our way to Harlan's Crossing?"

"I'm not, but you are."

"Why me?"

"I think it's imperative that we talk to Mr. Parker," Tower said. "I know he threw us out of the Big River Club, but he's got to know something about why his wife was murdered. I think I can get him to talk to me. I thought I could do that—he seems the kind of man more likely to talk man-to-man—and you could ride over to Harlan's Crossing. See if you can track down Jeffire, or the girl, or both."

"I don't mind that plan at all," Bird said. "I'm getting real tired of Big River."

Tower got to his feet. "I'm going for a walk, sometimes it helps me think. Care to join me?"

"I believe I'll stay here and see if this whiskey has any ideas."

Tower tipped his hat to her and left. She watched him leave the saloon, standing tall, with his broad shoulders and easy gait. He was a man very comfortable with himself.

Bird looked at the bottle.

Other people found their comfort outside themselves.

She poured another shot and drank.

Thirty-Six

The next morning, Bird stood before the Big River General Store, trying to forget about the dream she'd had: a woman with a pentagram carved into her chest was following her through the long grass near Killer's Draw. She hadn't slept well, and there was a crick in her neck. She rolled her head from side to side, trying to loosen up her neck muscles, and regretted passing on that second cup of coffee at the hotel restaurant.

Bird went inside, bought a few minimal provisions, mostly ammunition, then saddled up for her ride to Harlan's Crossing.

The morning was dull and gray; a thick sheen of metal spanned the sky, and the air was heavy and still. Bird tried to judge how quickly the layer might burn off, or if the thickness meant heavier weather was on the way.

She was glad for the respite from Big River. New country never meant anything really new to Bird, but at least it was different. In her opinion, people were the same everywhere regardless of location and typically expected the same of her by reputation.

It didn't matter to Bird.

She'd never encountered any type of situation she couldn't shoot her way out of.

Martha Jeffire had underestimated the amount of time it

took to get from Big River to Harlan's Crossing. Rather than a half day, Bird arrived in the late afternoon. She hadn't bothered to stop either, her lunch having been a bite of hardtack washed down with whiskey. A tension remained between her shoulder blades that the whiskey hadn't eased. But this was different from the morning neck ache she'd had, and even after the liberal application of alcohol, its failure to relax typically meant one thing: she was being followed. Despite pauses on the trail to look back over her route, Bird saw no sign of anyone coming after her—but that didn't necessarily mean anything.

For the time being, she ignored her suspicions and continued on into Harlan's Crossing.

Three saloons formed the nucleus of the town and Bird chose the one with the most horses in front, which meant the bar was mostly likely being actively tended. Unfortunately, it didn't mean the establishment served the best merchandise. But Bird would take a cheap, busy saloon over an expensive, unmanned bar any time. Hardworking bartenders were of utmost importance to serious drinkers.

Bird climbed down from her horse, looped the reins over the hitching post, and glanced back again toward the trail into town. She saw no signs of movement, but it wasn't like the desert where even one man on a horse would raise a small cloud of dust. She saw nothing but grass and mountains in the distance.

Still, the feeling was there, between her shoulders and creeping up toward the back of her neck.

She looked at the saloon, then noticed a general store next door. The whiskey was calling to her, but perhaps more than the sheriff or a popular bartender, the owner of a general store would know what was going on in town, and more important, whether Roger Jeffire had been by. Unlike her, she figured, Jeffire would start somewhere other than the saloon.

Bird made her way to the store and stepped inside. A man wearing a white apron over a blue shirt and peering through horn-rimmed glasses glanced up at her. He had a thick black pencil in his hand and had been squinting at a long, narrow sheet of yellow paper.

"Howdy," he said. "Help you?"

"I'm looking for two people," she said. "One is a reporter named Roger Jeffire from the *Big River Bugle* who would've come up here looking for a girl. The girl, now, she was supposedly seeing the young preacher who was murdered a couple weeks back. Have you seen Jeffire or know the girl?"

He made a checkmark on the sheet of paper with the pencil, then set both down.

"I don't," he said. "No reporter came by here, and believe me, if there was a girl in town who'd been seeing this preacher, I would've known about it. Big River isn't that far away and Harlan's Crossing isn't that big. We all heard about that killing—and the new one."

"I see," Bird said.

"If Jeffire had stopped by here but didn't talk to you, is there anyone or anywhere else he would have gone?"

The man thought for a moment and then shook his head. "No, sorry," he said.

Bird thanked him, left the store and went to the saloon. The place was about half full but the end of the bar was open, so Bird took up position there where she could see the whole saloon.

When the bartender came over, she ordered whiskey and asked him about Jeffire and the girl. The bartender had the same response as the general store owner: no sign of the reporter and no information about a girl who might have been involved with Egans.

Bird drank her whiskey and thought back to the meeting she and Tower had had with Martha Jeffire. Bird liked the woman but wondered if she had been telling them the whole story. But why lie? What benefit would she have to send them off on a wild goose chase?

She drank another whiskey and refilled her glass, trying to get the tension out from between her shoulders, but that nagging feeling wasn't going away. And Bird sensed that no matter how much good whiskey she poured down the hatch, something else was going to have to happen to put her mind at ease.

Bird thought again of the reporter. If Roger Jeffire hadn't come out to Harlan's Crossing, then where was he? And if there wasn't a girl from Harlan's Crossing who had been seeing Bertram Egans, why had Martha Jeffire said there was?

She nursed the questions in her mind, poured another whiskey, and a very simple answer appeared.

At the same time, two men pushed their way into the saloon.

One small. One big.

Henry Jones. And Mr. Seven.

Thirty-Seven

Mike Tower and Walter Morrison stood by the platform at the train station. There were a dozen people milling around, some with bags and others checking their pocket watches, wondering how much longer before loved ones would arrive.

Morrison had tracked down Tower and urged him to meet the afternoon train, which would be carrying a passenger of great interest. Tower had pressed for more information but Morrison hadn't divulged any additional tidbits.

They were several minutes early, and Tower studied the handbills posted along the ticket office's exterior walls. There were signs for a show that was coming to Big River, the usual advertisements for the saloons and land agents. There was also a sign warning rustlers and horse thieves to stay clear of Big River. The image on that one was a crude drawing of a man wearing a flour sack over his head with eye holes cut out.

"Yes, Big River has never had much of a problem with rustlers," Morrison said. "Unlike other boomtowns profiting from the cattle industry. I've heard stories of rustlers practically bankrupting a town with their thievery."

"So, how has Big River solved the problem?"

"Only one way to do it," Morrison said. "Like you mean it."

"You mean like this kind of thing?" Tower asked, gesturing toward the poster.

"That, and the harshness with which the guilty are treated. From what I understand, Big River has a reputation as a place cattle thieves avoid."

Tower was about to ask more, but in the distance, they heard the whistle of the train.

"Right on time," Morrison said.

The church secretary had been circumspect when Tower tried to find out who was arriving. He half wondered if Silas came out from San Francisco to see how the investigation was going. It would surprise him if that was the case, but then again, Big River had been full of surprises so far.

The train pulled into the main platform and the folks with luggage moved toward the cars, ignoring the fact that those on-board would have to disembark first. Tower and Morrison stood off to the side.

As passengers began to emerge from the train, Morrison walked forward, looking for the person he was expecting.

By now, Tower's curiosity was thoroughly piqued.

The stream of passengers exiting the train began to thin, until finally, one last group emerged. In the middle of that group, a woman stepped through the train doors. She was older, with stylish gray hair swept back beneath a floppy purple hat. Morrison approached her, said something, and then extended a hand that she took.

The woman stepped onto the platform and Morrison led her to Tower. Tower watched her walk toward him. She carried herself well, with excellent posture and square shoulders. The expression on her face wasn't haughty, however; if anything, it was open and welcoming.

Tower knew at once that he was going to like her.

"I will retrieve your suitcase, ma'am, while I leave you in the goods hands of Mr. Mike Tower," Morrison said.

He turned to Tower.

"Mr. Tower, I would like you to meet Evelyn Egans. Bertram's mother."

Thirty-Eight

"Ever rent out your shotgun?"

The bartender looked at Bird.

"Pardon me?" he asked.

"I know you've got one, probably a double-barrel, underneath the bar," Bird said. "I'm hoping it's loaded with double-aught buckshot."

The man refilled Bird's glass and looked at her. He had a square jaw and fierce green eyes that had seen plenty of bends in the trail. He moved down the bar and poured drinks for two other customers who had just come into the saloon.

Bird drank her whiskey in one smooth pull and licked her lips after it went down. She had been mulling over her options ever since her old friends had entered the bar and made a point of not looking her way.

It was clearly her move.

The bartender finished with his customers and slowly made his way back to Bird, wiping down the bar on his return trip.

"I can see you've got two guns already. What do you need a third for?"

Bird smiled. "Most of the time, the firepower I bring to a party is more than enough to do the job. But occasionally, I come face-to-face with bigger game. The kind that that can eat a couple of .45s and keep coming. For those unpleasant creatures, I need something that'll bring them down without too much trouble. Your shotgun, for instance."

"The thing is, I don't want 'my' shotgun to get me into trouble. Even if someone else is using it."

"Believe me, that shotgun and I will be keeping whatever happens between us."

"I don't want any trouble here in the saloon," he finally said.

"You won't get any from me," she said. "Especially if you rent me that shotgun right now."

She had already done the calculations in her head. There was no way she was going to try to ride back to Big River tonight. She'd bunk up in Harlan's Crossing—there had to be a room somewhere, and head back in the morning. But she had a pretty good idea that she could expect company tonight. A part of her was impressed with the brazen manner in which Henry Jones and Mr. Seven made no attempts to conceal their presence.

They wanted her to know they were here.

Daring her to do something.

Bird laid ten dollars on the bar.

"For the shotgun and a bottle of whiskey. I'll bring the shotgun back but not the bottle."

He got her the whiskey first, then brought the shotgun out from underneath the bar. It looked ugly and totally utilitarian. Just greasy, worn wood on the stock, and a dark barrel that had never seen a rag and a bottle of polish. It looked exactly like what a bartender's shotgun should look like.

She took it from him and Bird figured it was good deal for him—he probably had another one stashed somewhere.

The gun was sawed off but still impressive in its heft.

"Need more shells?" the bartender asked.

Bird shook her head. "If I can't do it with two, more won't help."

She grabbed the bottle and the shotgun, and walked past Henry Jones and Mr. Seven without looking at them.

Bird figured she'd see them soon enough.

Thirty-Nine

The three of them sat in the parlor at Mrs. Wolfe's Boarding-house. Mrs. Egans had insisted on heading directly there, where-upon she deposited her luggage in Bertram's former room, freshened up, and met Tower and Morrison for afternoon tea.

Tower had received a chilly reception from Mrs. Wolfe, but he ignored her obvious distaste at his presence. The woman seemed to relax her negative attitude toward Mrs. Egans, al-though clearly she was a bit put off.

Now, they sank into their respective chairs around the fire-place. There was wood in the hearth, but it hadn't been lit, as the day was still warm. Mrs. Egans set her teacup on the black lacquered table that was between the chairs, then folded her hands in her lap.

"I suppose the shock has worn off," she said, answering Morrison's question as to her general condition. "Now all that's left is sadness. Bertram did not have an easy life. I thought he had finally found his way with his religion, and it certainly seemed that he had. Now this."

Tower wondered about what kind of reception the wom-an would receive from the townspeople of Big River. He hoped they would temper their obvious disdain for the wom-an's dead son.

Mrs. Egans' refinement came as a bit of a surprise to Tower. Judging by her letters, he had not expected the woman now in front of him to speak with such a deep and richly cultured voice.

"I made arrangements to come as soon as the news reached me," she said. "But even a woman like me with a simple life can encounter complications with getting away for an extended period of time. It took more planning that I would have thought."

"How were you notified?" Tower asked. "About Bertram?"

"Father Silas sent word."

She sighed, picked up her teacup, and sipped as Tower wondered if the woman knew he was in possession of her letters. He considered telling her and offering to return them but something held him back.

"May I ask why you ultimately decided to come to Big River?" Tower asked.

"I felt I owed him that, Mr. Tower," the woman said. "I may not have been there for him at certain points in his life, but I felt that we had made a tentative connection again and that our bond was healing. I wanted to be here for him now, even though he is gone."

She set down her teacup a bit too firmly on the table. The sound seemed to startle her.

"Have they found the person responsible?" she asked.

Tower glanced at Morrison, who caught the nonverbal suggestion that he answer the question.

"The short answer is that they have not caught your son's killer," Morrison said. "Yet."

"Somehow, I knew that would be the answer," she said. "I assume that would have been the first thing you would have told me."

"I wish we were able to give you that good news," Tower said.

"You should know, Mrs. Egans, that the investigation is continuing," Morrison said. "In fact, Father Silas has asked Mr. Tower here to look into it as well."

"Are the local authorities not up to the job?"

Morrison shifted uncomfortably in his chair.

"The local authorities are doing the best they can," Tower said. "However, before I answered my calling, I worked for some time as an investigator. I believe Silas thought I might be able to help. And if not, he may have simply sent me out here for a second opinion."

"It doesn't sound like there is a first opinion yet, though; am I correct?"

Smart woman, Tower thought.

"That's correct," he said.

Forty

Bird was surprised by the patience displayed by Henry Jones and Mr. Seven. When she hunkered down in her room in Harlan's Crossing, she figured they would come for her around midnight or so. In their minds, that would have given her plenty of time to get even more drunk and then pass out, dead to the world. At which time, they could make her dead to the real world.

But they hadn't made their move by one o'clock in the morning.

They actually waited until three.

And when they arrived, they did it in style. There was the faintest creaking of floorboards just outside her door, followed by a scrape then a thunderous crash as the door was knocked completely off its hinges. The door fell forward amid shouts and grunts and dark shadows accompanied by a cacophony of gunfire. Bullets exploded all around Bird, but she held steady until she could make out the clear definition of a man, then unloaded both barrels from the rented shotgun, figuring the man assigned the door-breaking task would be Mr. Seven.

She was wrong.

The double-aught shot obliterated the first man in, painting the wall behind him with an explosion of dark blood. But Bird had caught a glimpse of the man's face and recognized him to be one of the two men she'd seen in the restaurant while defending herself from the man calling himself Ronald Hale.

Dammit, she thought.

Bird tossed aside the shotgun, drew both pistols and shot the next man through the door, who turned out to be the first man's dining companion from the restaurant.

And then two things happened.

Henry Jones darted into the room, and flattened himself against the wall, with his hands up.

Bird drew a bead on him.

"I'm not here to hurt you," he shouted.

This statement was followed by an explosion of glass that showered Bird with lacerating fragments. She hesitated for just a moment before shooting Henry Jones with her left pistol, putting a bullet dead center in his forehead. And then Mr. Seven was through the window and across the room, grabbing her right arm and throwing her through the window. Bird had the sensation of being caught in a ferocious wind, the walls around her blurring with speed, a pain in her shoulder, and then she was being heaved over the narrow walkway and cast-iron railing, down two stories before she landed flat on her back in the street. The impact was brutal, driving all of the air from her lungs. Bird gasped, struggling to breathe.

She saw blackness and stars. Whether it was the sky or the blanket of pain and shock that she felt throughout her body she could not decide. She clenched her left hand. It was empty. She clenched her right. The gun butt was still there.

Bird blinked and rolled onto her left side, happy to see that she really had been staring at the sky, and now the images of a dirt street from ground level and distorted buildings on either side took shape in her vision.

Along with the foot of Mr. Seven crashing into her stomach.

The pain was all-consuming and fierce, and her mouth was suddenly full of blood. She felt no fear or panic, just pain and the sensation of something kicking against the palm of her right hand. She then realized that although she was firing her pistol over and over, the hammer was clacking on empty chambers. Her view of the street was replaced by the face of Mr. Seven.

With the top of his head gone.

Bird couldn't breathe, the air was still refusing to enter her lungs, and her mouth was full of blood.

She smiled, and blood poured from her mouth.

She had cut down Mr. Seven.

Turned him into Mr. Three and a Half.

Forty-One

Tower thought about Mrs. Egans. Morrison said he would help the woman get settled, then give her a quick tour of Big River so she could make her way around on her own. Mrs. Egans hadn't mentioned how long she planned on staying in Big River, and neither he nor Morrison felt the need to ask. Tower figured the answer would be that she was going to stay as long as she needed to, which was the way Tower was approaching this case, as well.

Tower walked back into the main street of Big River. He thought the woman was holding up pretty well. A child dying had to be every parent's worst nightmare.

If nothing else, maybe the woman could get closure, as long as Tower found out who was responsible for her son's murder. But he didn't feel an overwhelming sense of confidence with regard to the investigation. It seemed like every day brought new questions instead of answers. And the old questions hadn't been answered yet either.

Tower thought back to his first time reading through the papers Silas had given him. He had come to a decision regarding the documents he had studied on the train and continued to read. He would go back to his hotel room, pore over everything one more time, box them up, and give them to Mrs. Egans tomorrow. Once he had learned everything he could, he no longer had a need for them—and she was the rightful owner. It wouldn't be right to keep them any longer.

He couldn't help but think, however, that an answer was still somewhere to be found in those notes and letters. Something that he had overlooked. The thought nagged at him, irritating him and leaving behind a sense of frustration.

As he continued his walk, Tower shook off his negative thoughts and took a deep breath. The night was alive in Big River. A herd had come in earlier in the day, the cowboys had been paid, and laughter, shouting, and music poured out of the saloons. Occasionally, a gunshot could be heard.

He thought of years back when he would have been in there, a drink in his hand and a gun on his hip. Spoiling for a fight, a chance to work out the anger he felt inside by delivering pain to a complete stranger.

He was glad to no longer be a part of it. He had come to terms with his own pain, his own past, and no longer felt the need to demand answers from people who had no hope of providing them.

Tower's thoughts were interrupted by the sudden appearance of a rider at the end of the street. The white on the horse's chest caught Tower's eye. He knew the horse and he knew the rider.

He raced ahead, caught the Appaloosa by the reins and pulled Bird from the saddle. Even in the dark, he could see the blood on her face, the way she slumped forward, the dark stains on the front of her chest. He quickly looked for signs of an obvious gunshot wound but found none.

Tower lifted her, remembered where the doctor's office was, and carried her easily in his arms, running down the street until he turned a corner and spotted the medical sign in the window.

He kicked at the door with his foot and was nearly ready to kick it in when someone partially opened it from within.

The face of a young woman, her brown hair pinned back behind her ears, took in the sight of Bird and immediately stepped back, opening the door wider.

"Tower," Bird said. Her voice was soft and he looked at her face. Her eyes were glazed and unfocused.

"Shh," Tower said.

The woman gestured for Tower to come inside, and pointed to a table in the center of the room.

He crossed over to it, set Bird down as gently as possible, and leaned down toward her face.

"Tower," she said again.

The woman who'd opened the door moved behind the table and lit two brass oil lamps. The room brightened considerably as an older man appeared in the doorway.

"Just breathe," Tower said to Bird.

"Jeffire," she whispered.

She started coughing. More blood trickled from the corner of her mouth.

The doctor appeared next to Tower. "Well, that coughing doesn't sound very promising," he said. "You're going to have to step aside, young man. Frannie and I will take over from here."

"Tower," Bird said. "Martha Jeffire. She lied to us. I think he's there."

"That's enough!" the doctor said, as he pulled Bird's gun belt from her hips and his assistant began cutting away Bird's shirt.

"Frannie, get me some whiskey," the doctor said.

Tower looked at Bird.

"My kind of doc," she said, smiling, and then her eyes closed.

Forty-Two

Martha Jeffire opened the door upon Tower's knock.

"Oh," she said. "I wasn't expecting you."

"I just need to talk to you about something," Tower said. "It won't take very long."

She stepped aside, and shuffled uncertainly. Tower noted that she didn't have the same quiet composure she'd shown on his last visit.

"If you have any of that coffee, I would greatly appreciate it," Tower said, trying to put her at ease. "I remember it from the last time I was here. Thankfully, you forced a cup on me and I still recall how good it was."

"I've just started a pot," she said.

"We'll definitely need some," Tower said. "I'm afraid I've got some bad news."

Tower sat at the table. When the coffee was ready, Martha Jeffire poured him a cup, set it on the table in front of him, then sat down in the opposite chair.

"Let me be as direct as I can possibly be," Tower said. "I believe I have found your husband's body."

The lie came out of his mouth as easy as he could deliver it. He knew that Martha Jeffire wouldn't believe him. But he just needed a small amount of time.

"What do you mean, his body?" she asked.

Tower ignored the question and said, "I need to draw a map of where I found him," he said. "Do you have a pencil and paper?"

Martha Jeffire looked at him for a brief moment, then fetched a yellow ledger with a black fountain pen.

Tower wrote, *Where are they?* As he said, "This is roughly where I rode today."

He handed her the pen.

She wrote, *In the pantry behind the kitchen*, and he said, "And it was right about here, between this valley and this river."

He wrote on the paper, *How many?*

She held up one finger.

"That coffee was so good I could use another cup," he said. "And then I can show you exactly where I found him."

As she got up and went to the kitchen Tower followed her, grabbing the pot of hot coffee. He slipped past Martha Jeffire, opened the door to the pantry and threw the coffee directly into the face of a cowboy who was sitting on top of a bound Roger Jeffire. The cowboy had a pistol in his holster and a dime-store novel in his hands.

The scalding coffee burned his face and he screamed, dropped the book, and covered his face. He shot to his feet, planning to run into the kitchen, Tower assumed. So Tower kneed him in the groin, then whipped a vicious uppercut that smashed into the man's mouth, splitting his lips and knocking several teeth onto the floor.

Tower grabbed him by the collar and dragged him from the pantry, took away his gun and pistol-whipped him. The blow knocked the man unconscious and he landed on his face on the kitchen floor.

Martha Jeffire used a paring knife to cut her husband free and remove the gag from his mouth.

"Thank you," he said to Tower. He hugged Martha, who had begun to cry. "We don't have much time," Jeffire said. "We have to get to the *Bugle* office. Now."

Forty-Three

"Can't you just tell me?" Tower asked as they ran toward the newspaper office. Jeffire ran with a wobble and massaged his wrists where the ropes had bound him.

"It's a very big story," Jeffire huffed. "It would be much faster for you to see some of what I've found, and then I can fill in the rest of the details. Plus," he said. "If I didn't show you, you probably wouldn't believe it."

They emerged from the side street onto the town's commercial block.

"Is Martha going to be all right?" Tower asked. They had walked Jeffire's wife over to a neighbor's and given her a gun. The neighbor had been a cavalry officer and knew how to handle a weapon.

"She'll be fine," Jeffire said. "They only got me because we were surprised. They won't catch us off guard again."

"Who were they?" Tower asked.

But Jeffire was done talking, and the two men took a circuitous route toward the newspaper's office.

A group of cowboys had spilled out of a saloon into the street. Two were fighting, although to Tower it looked more like a drunken wrestling match than fisticuffs.

He and Jeffire skirted the crowd and soon reached the headquarters of the *Big River Bugle*.

The sounds of late-night drinkers shouting and cavorting filled the air, and in the distance they could hear the cattle bawling in their pens, protesting their newfound confinement.

Jeffire fumbled in his pockets for a key, his hands shaking. Tower worried about the man collapsing. He himself was out of breath, and he leaned his back against a stout wooden pole that helped support the overhanging roof.

Jeffire cursed under his breath as he struggled with the keys.

Somewhere, a door opened then closed, and Tower cocked his head. It had sounded like it came from the other side of the building. But the only door on the other side of the building was the door to the *Bugle*.

"Could there be someone else—" he began to say to Jeffire but just then the journalist turned the key in the lock and the entire night lit up in a blinding flash of white.

Tower felt himself flung backward as something immense and powerful hit him with a force unlike anything he'd ever felt before.

He had the sudden sense that he was airborne and all of the night sounds were gone, replaced by utter and complete silence.

And then he was on the ground, stunned, his body a confusing mixture of pain and numbness. Tower thought of Jeffire, of how the man had been right in the front of the door while he, Tower, had been behind that post.

The idea that Jeffire might not have survived hit him like another blow, as the memory of the door opening and closing rushed back at him. Someone had been inside, waiting for them.

Tower thought about Bird back at the doctor's office and how he might soon be joining her there.

The smell of smoke surrounded him, along with shouts of people spilling out into the street.

He recognized something about the smell of that smoke. Something mixed in that he'd gotten to know a long time ago when he had briefly worked in a mine.

The scent was unmistakable.

Dynamite.

EPISODE FOUR

Forty-Four

"You've got a problem, young lady," the doctor said. Bird was oddly captivated, either by his bright-green eyes and their intensity, or the compassion that was on full display. Whichever it was, it was a sentiment she wasn't accustomed to having directed at her.

"Don't we all, Doc?" Bird asked.

Bird glanced at the young woman on the other side of the table. The doctor's daughter, she assumed. The thin, pale girl paid no attention to Bird as she methodically stocked the doctor's medical kit.

"When I saw all that blood on your front, I was certain you had been shot, most likely by a shotgun," the doctor said. "Much to my surprise, you didn't have a mark on you, other than some bruises on your side, some shallow lacerations, and a few deeper cuts from glass. As I understand it, you were thrown through a window?"

"Through a window, and over a second-floor balcony," Bird said. "It was a rather unpleasant evening."

"So, then I wondered," the doctor continued. "Where did all this blood come from?"

Bird sat up.

"I believe I'll be on my way, now," she said.

The doctor put a hand on her shoulder as she began to get to her feet. Ordinarily, Bird despised anyone touching her, but for some reason, her temper didn't flare with the old doctor.

"Not so fast, young lady," he said. "I figured out the source of that bleeding." He pointed toward Bird's stomach. "It's coming from right in there."

Bird pushed his hand away and got to her feet.

"That's an interesting theory," Bird said.

She snatched her gun belt off a hook by the door and shrugged it on around her hips.

"I heard a rumor," the doctor said, "that a certain Bird Hitchcock was in town. A woman as famous for her drinking as for her ability with a pair of those." He pointed at the guns Bird was now tying down to her legs.

"Well you shouldn't believe everything you hear," Bird said. "Didn't they teach you that in medical school?"

"I suspect it's the drinking," the doctor continued. "You're shredding your insides."

Bird was about to respond when the door banged open.

Two men carried in the body of Roger Jeffire, while a second set of men carried in Mike Tower.

Jeffire was unconscious; Tower's eyes were open and focused on Bird.

Bird looked at Tower.

"What the hell are you doing here?" she asked.

Forty-Five

Tower awoke in the morning after a long and mostly sleepless night. He'd tossed and turned, alternately feeling dizzy and nauseated from the explosion, which caused a constant ringing in his head that increased and decreased in intensity with every restless turn.

Now, the pounding in his head was finally gone and though exhausted, he felt steady.

The bed was actually one of four glorified cots in a small room in the doctor's house, located next door to the actual doctor's office. The other three beds were empty. On the wall was a painting of a flower, with deftly defined shadows that bespoke of talent. Tower wondered who had painted it.

He stood, steadied himself as a mild wave of dizziness came and went, put his clothes on, and left the room.

The doctor was sitting at his desk. He looked up at Tower's entrance.

"Frannie!" the doctor called out. The young woman who assisted the doctor hurried into the room.

"Find the pain medicine for Mr. Tower," he said. Then he looked at Tower.

"Have a seat on the table, preacher," the doctor said. "You aren't going anywhere until I say so."

Tower hesitated, then sat on the table, feeling a bit relieved to sit down after the long trek of ten feet from the spare room the doctor's table. He knew he was a long way from feeling like himself.

The doctor stood in front of Tower and looked at Tower's eyes.

"You were knocked unconscious and judging by your condition last night, I would guess that you suffered a concussion."

"Wonderful," Tower said.

The young woman reentered with a tiny glass bottle containing a brown liquid.

"It's good," the doctor said as he took it from her and handed it to Tower. "I mix it up myself."

Tower slipped the bottle into his pocket.

"Your pupils appear normal," the doctor said, "and I see no signs of lingering problems. How do you feel?"

"I feel fine. Just a little tired."

"That's to be expected. Get plenty of rest for the next few days and you should be fine. Take a sip of that syrup as needed. Just don't drink it all at once."

Tower hesitated and then looked around the room.

"What happened to Jeffire?" he asked.

The doctor shook his head. "He didn't make it. It appears he took the brunt of the blast. Were you standing behind him?"

"No, I was standing behind a post."

"It must have protected you. Jeffire wasn't so lucky."

Tower got to his feet, a bit unsteady.

"Go back to the hotel. Rest. Forget about all of this nonsense going on in town," the doctor said, waving his hand in the general direction of Main Street. "All of that can wait."

Tower went to the door.

"I'm not so sure it can, doctor."

Forty-Six

"You sure know how to have a good time without me," Bird said.

They stood in front of the remains of the *Big River Bugle*. The outline of the structure was still there, but everything inside was gone. What hadn't been destroyed by the blast had been consumed in the ensuing fire. A pile of charred lumber occupied the former site of the newspaper's office and the air was ripe with the smell that reminded Bird of a freshly doused campfire.

She turned and looked at Tower. He was pale, but standing straight.

"How are you feeling?" she asked.

"Fine. You?"

"Fine," she said. "Now that we're both done lying to each other, what the hell are we going to do?"

He didn't answer and Bird looked at the saloon that was two doors down. She stretched and felt a pain in her ribs. The doctor had told her he didn't think they were broken, but they still hurt like hell. A few glasses of whiskey would make the pain go away and an entire bottle would make her forget she'd even been hurt in the first place. And forgetting hurts was what whiskey was all about.

"I'm going to—"

Before she could finish what she was about to say, a woman's voice called out.

"Here, take this."

Bird looked over Tower's shoulder as he turned to face Martha Jeffire.

If it was possible, the woman looked even worse than they did. Her hair was in disarray, her dress was dirty, and her eyes were disorganized and unfocused.

Martha Jeffire had a battered envelope in her hand. Behind her, a horse and buckboard were piled high with a couple of suitcases and some furniture, all of it looking as if it had been gathered and loaded with great abandon.

Tower moved to embrace her but she held up her hand.

"I'm leaving," she said and thrust the papers to Tower.

"My deepest prayers—" he started to say.

"I'm leaving now," she repeated, cutting him off.

"Where are you going?" he asked.

"Back home to Kansas," she said. "There's no reason for me to stay here. I don't believe in God so I won't be staying for the burial. I hate this place and all it stands for."

Bird saw Tower look down at the papers in his hands.

"I'm sorry about your husband," Bird said quickly, before the woman could cut her off.

Martha Jeffire shrugged her shoulders. "I always knew there was a chance we wouldn't grow old together," she said. "Roger took too many risks, no matter how often I tried to ride herd on him. Mind you, I'm not blaming him, that's just who he was."

She didn't wait for a response, just turned and walked back toward her buckboard.

Tower looked down at the envelope in his hand.

"If you need me, I'll be getting medical treatment in bottle form," Bird said. "Doctor's orders."

Forty-Seven

Bird sat on the front porch of the hotel with her feet up on the railing and a bottle of whiskey in her lap. The sun was setting, and she figured the best way to watch night fall over Big River was to sit here and drink to the end of the day.

Her body was recovering as the aches and pains of being thrown out of a second-floor window were fading now, aided in no small part by the liquor. Her mind was at ease. Tower was off doing something with Jesus she guessed; probably trying his best to make sure Roger Jeffire was allowed into heaven. Bird wondered if Tower would do the same for her. Probably, but she had a fairly good idea that instead of being surrounded by angels in the afterlife, she would be surrounded by dirt.

Bird drank from the bottle, loving the way the liquor felt as it worked its way through her body. That doctor didn't know what he was talking about. She felt fine. One day they'd probably recognize her as the medical marvel she knew herself to be.

Bird's mind drifted and she found herself thinking back to her drink at the Big River Club. There was something about that place; something that kept irritating her and she couldn't figure out why. All those pompous men sitting in their private club with pictures of themselves on the wall . . .

Bird sat up straight, dropped her feet onto the hotel's porch.

The goddamn pictures.

Bird jumped to her feet, got her horse, and shot over to the Big River Club. She hitched the Appaloosa to the rail, then pushed her way through the front door and headed for the bar.

"Whiskey and a beer chaser," she said to the young bartender. He was a peach-faced young man with corresponding fuzz on his chin.

He looked at her and hesitated, then poured the whiskey and fetched a beer.

"You have to be a member to drink here, but I know who you are," he said, his voice surprisingly deep and robust. "I figure it would be easier to serve you than to try to throw you out of here, Miss Bird Hitchcock."

He beamed with pride at his cleverness.

"Smart man," she said.

She tossed the whiskey back and carried her beer with her to the wall. It was a collage of rough sketches, a few pictures of the important people of the club—Mr. Parker being at the top—and a few others.

Bird had spotted the collage when she and Tower burst in just after Mrs. Parker's murder, but had merely glanced at the display.

Now she knew what had been bothering her.

It was a picture near the bottom of three men standing near a trophy elk they had shot. Their names were written under each.

The man on the far right was familiar to Bird.

He had called himself Ronald Hale.

But the name under his picture said something else.

Martin Branson.

Forty-Eight

Tower went back to the hotel and debated about opening the envelope from Martha Jeffire. But instead, he collected the papers that Silas had given him regarding Bertram Egans and set out for Mrs. Wolfe's Boardinghouse. Now that he was done with them, he wanted to return the letters to Evelyn Egans as soon as possible. Maybe they would help bring some sort of closure for the woman until the murderer of her son was brought to justice.

He crossed the street, passed the Conway brothers' law office, when just ahead of him a door opened. Tower stepped aside as Evelyn Egans emerged from the Big River Land Office. She seemed startled by the sight of him.

"Oh!" she said. "Sorry for almost hitting you with the door."

"Actually, it was a stroke of luck. I was looking for you," he said.

"I was heading back to my room . . ."

"This won't take more than a minute or two," he said.

They sat down on a bench near the door, and Tower handed the thick bundle of paper to her.

"This is what Silas gave me when he asked me to look into the murder of your son," Tower said. "It's a collection of papers that includes letters from you to Silas, as well as some of the original documents Bertram supplied upon his application to the church. I think you should have them."

"Oh, dear," she said. Tower watched as she held the papers, running a hand over the surface with reverence and glancing at the first few pages inside.

"They were fairly informative to me," Tower said, "and helped me get off to a quick start in the investigation. But obviously, I've still got a lot of work to do in finding out what happened."

"Are you sure you don't need them anymore?" Mrs. Egans asked. "I mean, I'm not sure if they will bring me any comfort. In fact, they might do just the opposite." Her shoulders sagged and she looked away from Tower.

"No, I've gleaned everything I can. And any information that I for certain wanted to remember I copied down. These are yours. I think Bertram would have wanted you to have them."

She nodded, lifted the papers in her arm, and held them against her chest. She then stood and turned directly to Tower.

"Thank you for these," she said. "Now I will—"

"Rose Sutton! I'll be damned!"

Tower and Evelyn Egans both turned to see a cowboy, older in years but wearing the chaps and spurs of a working drover, standing in the street looking at them with a huge grin on his face.

"Rosie! It's me! Hank Durfen from Dodge City!"

Tower turned to Mrs. Egans. Her face was rigid.

"I'm sorry but you have me confused with someone else," she said.

The drover looked at her out of the corner of his eye.

"I don't think so, ma'am. Your cabaret show last year was the highlight of my life!" he practically guffawed. "Especially, when you personally thanked me for tossing out some unruly fans. I'd recognize that pretty face of yours anywhere!"

"I'm sorry, sir, but you are mistaken," she said, then turned to Tower.

"I'm afraid I'm very uncomfortable and will be going now."

She walked away, her heels banging so hard on the wooden boards they sounded like rifle shots.

The old cowboy looked at Tower.

"I'll be damned! And I haven't even started drinking yet!"

Forty-Nine

Bird stood in front of the pictures of Big River Club members and shook her head. What was it with men needing to endlessly honor each other? Why couldn't they just do what had to be done and leave it at that? Deeds done throughout your life earned their own honor, good or bad. Take Bird, for instance. She'd never once sought out fortune or fame but it—or maybe it was infamy—had found her.

Another tintype caught her eye. Among a group of about a dozen men—all armed to the teeth—was Ronald Hale, or as she now knew him to be, Martin Branson. What had they been, a posse? Bird recognized Mr. Parker, and the two attorney brothers Tower had pointed out. She looked for any more information, but it was a display of bravado and weaponry, not much else.

Bird went back to the bar and ordered another whiskey and a beer from the young bartender.

"Did you like our picture gallery?" the bartender asked. "The club is very proud of it. It's the biggest collection of those newfangled things in the whole state."

Bird could tell he liked her and was trying to impress her, and not just because of her reputation. She decided to use his obvious interest to her advantage.

"Very impressive," she said. "What's the story behind everyone carrying five or six guns apiece, posing like they'd just captured a passel of outlaws?"

"Oh, that one," the bartender said. Bird noticed a slight change in his demeanor. He suddenly seemed unsure of himself. "They were just having fun in that one. You know, dressing up for the camera, that kind of thing."

Bird knew a lie when she heard it, but she moved on.

"I had no idea my old friend Martin Branson lived here in Big River," she said. "We punched cows together one summer back in Texas. He's as tough as old saddle leather."

"You know Branson?" the bartender asked. His friendly demeanor was back and he sounded slightly relieved now that she'd steered the conversation away from the picture. "He was one of the founders of this club. Wish he'd stop in more often. He's always got a few tall tales to tell."

"I miss those stories," Bird said. "He always said he wanted to start breeding horses. Did he ever make that dream come true?"

"Horses?" the bartender asked. "No, he never said anything about horses. He had a ranch but he sold it to Mr. Parker for a lot of money. He negotiated a small cabin at the western end of the range where he runs a few head, mostly for beef and spending money. Mr. Parker really made it worth his while to sell. He's a lucky man, really carved out a nice life for himself."

Bird drank the whiskey and then chugged the beer.

"Thank you for the conversation," she said.

"I'll tell Branson you said hello," the bartender offered.

"I appreciate it, but I expect he and I will be crossing paths sooner than later."

Fifty

"Absolutely," Morrison said. "My space is yours."

Tower stood with the church secretary in the narrowly confined but functional church office. For some reason, his instinct had told him not to study Jeffire's information in his hotel room. And the only office he knew of where he would be welcomed was Walter Morrison's.

"Thank you, I appreciate it," he said.

"Does this have to do with your investigation?"

"Maybe, maybe not." Tower saw no reason in getting anyone's hopes up, least of all his own.

Morrison provided Tower with paper and writing implements, then showed him where a small coffee pot was located should he need something to help him with his analysis.

He sat down, opened the folder, and pulled out the sheaf of papers.

It was much thinner than he thought it would be. Apparently, some of the thickness had been the envelope, not the contents inside.

The first sheet contained about a page full of neat, tight script that appeared masculine to his eye. Tower figured it was Jeffire's own hand.

The entire thing was in quotations, with a heading that read "Parker speech."

Tower read the undated transcript. It had to do with the threat of cattle rustling on the future prosperity of Big River.

The main thrust of Parker's speech seemed to Tower to be a call for ordinary citizens to share in the responsibility of the town's future. One sentence in particular had been underlined: "I hereby establish a community protocol; that being the absolute necessity of every individual to do whatever is necessary, to take whatever action the situation calls for, whether it's peaceful or violent, to protect each other's lives, businesses, and property."

Tower finished reading the rest of the speech, which amounted to a long, highly optimistic vision for the future of Big River.

The second paper was a newspaper clipping from the *Pennsylvania Inquirer*. The brief article described the arrest of a prostitute named Francine Pascal who had been running a house of ill repute. Local authorities were reported to have shut down the business and arrested her.

The third piece was another, shorter article that simply stated Francine Pascal had been released from prison and her whereabouts were unknown.

That was it. Tower picked up the thick envelope and shook it to make sure there was nothing else inside.

There wasn't.

Tower shook his head.

As had been the case all along, his investigation was raising more questions than it was providing answers.

He hoped that trend would reverse.

And soon.

Fifty-One

The western edge of the Parker ranch would not be a particularly small chunk of real estate, Bird knew. People in town deferred to him as if he owned most of Big River. She wondered how Sheriff Chesser was doing with the investigation into Mrs. Parker's murder. Not very well, she guessed. Something told her, though, that the entire town was looking for the woman's killer, while she and Tower were the sole investigators of Bertram Egans' killing.

The Appaloosa picked her way up a rocky incline and they topped out on a rise overlooking an immense valley. Word was the Parker Ranch comprised some twenty-thousand head of cattle and well more than quintuple that in acreage.

She knew that the south end of his ranch was established by a thin ridgeline called Bison Ridge that funneled down to the western edge where it met Sweetwater Creek. It took her most of the morning to find where the two landforms met, and then she turned north, ranging back and forth as she made her way up the edge of the ranch.

Several hours later, she heard screams.

Bird brought her horse to a stop, and together they waited. She could tell the sounds weren't human and since they were in the middle of cattle country, she assumed they were cows. But she'd occasionally worked as a ranch hand and knew how everything worked, from branding to castrating to birthing, and she could tell that these weren't the normal bawling of cattle. This was something much more painful.

She nudged the Appaloosa ahead. They climbed a low hill and crossed the summit, from where Bird spotted a weathered log cabin sitting in a lonesome canyon. A few hundred yards from the cabin, a man had a roaring fire going, and Bird could see the branding irons being heated in the center of the flames. Beyond the fire, a holding corral with driftwood logs serving as fence railings penned in a few dozen cattle.

A cow was on the ground, with the man leaning over its haunch, burning a brand into its side.

But the way he was doing it told Bird a different story. As she watched, he got off the cow, undid the rope, and kicked the cow repeatedly until it got to its feet. As the cow stood, its legs shaking, the man kicked it again.

Bird ground her teeth together. The West had never been a place that held humane treatment of animals to a high standard. The fact was, cowboys were some of the cruelest men she'd ever met when it came to animals.

She rode down to the fire, making no pretense as to her intentions. The man turned upon her approach and Bird recognized the man who had called himself Ronald Hale, but whose name was most likely Martin Branson.

Bird saw him glance over to the log cabin where a Winchester leaned near the door.

Too far away now.

"Well hello, Mr. Hale. Or should I say, Mr. Branson?"

"I suggest you leave my property right now if you know

what's good for you," he said. He looked Bird directly in the eye, then glanced away at the rifle.

"Awfully far away, isn't it?" Bird asked.

"What do you want?" he asked.

"You can start by telling me why you're torturing these cattle."

"It's called branding, you stupid bitch," he said.

A coolness filled Bird's belly. She had clearly underestimated the creature standing before her and she now looked at Martin Branson in a new light.

She swung down from the Appaloosa and approached him. Behind him, the cattle stood nervously, perturbed by the smell of the fire and the screams. Most of them pressed against the opposite side of the fence, as far away as they could get from Branson and the smell of smoke.

"Branding, huh?" she asked. "That's what you call it?"

A sneer crossed Branson's face. "What, is the famous Bird Hitchcock going to shoot me because I lied to her?"

"Why did you go through that whole charade?" she asked. "I'm curious. And you did it with such gusto—you really got into the part, didn't you?"

Branson sighed like he was tired of the conversation.

Bird drew her gun and shot him in the foot.

Branson screamed, toppled onto his back, and writhed on the ground. Bird walked past him, found the rope he'd used to tie up the cow, picked it up, went back to Branson, and kicked him in the ribs.

He howled, one hand on his ribs, the other trying to reach his bloody foot.

Bird used her boot to roll him onto his stomach and then put a knee in his back and tied his arms behind him. He struggled against her, but she ground her knee directly into his spine, then stepped back and kicked him in the ribs again, this time hard enough to flop him onto his back.

"He's going to kill you, you dirty whore!" Branson yelled. Flecks of foam were on his lips, and his face was red. The leg with the damaged foot was twitching.

"Dirty whore?" Bird asked. "I resent that as I bathe regularly and take pride in my appearance."

Bird went to the fire, pulled out one of the branding irons, studied the glowing red tip, and walked back to Martin Branson.

"No!" he shouted.

"It's called branding, you stupid bitch," she said and then jammed the tip of the brand into the side of Branson's face.

He screamed again, and struggled to get to his feet. Bird stepped back and kicked him in the face, her boot catching the tip of his jaw and snapping his head back.

Branson plopped back onto the ground.

He was whimpering.

"Who hired you to come to the hotel and tell me that Bertram Egans killed your daughter? You know, the daughter that doesn't actually exist."

Branson let out an incoherent string of words that may or may not have included curse words.

Bird stepped around him, spotted the burn wound on his face, and kicked him square on the damaged flesh. The toe of her boot caught and pulled a chunk of charred meat out of his cheek.

"It's called telling the truth, you dirty whore," Bird said.

"You're going to kill me anyway," he said. Tears streamed down his face and gobs of spit hung from his lips.

"You're a real mess, Mr. Branson. But I'm probably not go-ing to kill you, even though you deserve it. I may just spare your life, on one condition," Bird said. "As long as you tell me the name. I just want one name."

Branson stopped squirming, went still, and finally gave her the name.

Bird walked to the cabin, took the Winchester, then went to the makeshift corral and freed all of the animals. Then she kicked dirt over the fire and heaved the branding irons into the trees behind the cabin.

She walked back to Branson, jacked a shell into the Win-chester's chamber, and put the muzzle next to his temple.

"You know how I said I wouldn't kill you?"

He didn't answer.

She pulled the trigger.

"You're not the only one who can act."

Fifty-Two

According to the hotel's proprietor, Joseph Parker spent the most hours of his days between an office at the Wyoming Cattlemen's Association office, and the Big River Club, conveniently located two blocks from each other. Tower figured Parker had ceded the day-to-day responsibilities of his ranch to someone else, possibly a family member or a longtime employee. It sounded like he was enjoying the good life in town.

The WCA building was stout and formidable, probably meant to represent the reputations of the men who headed the organization. Two stories, wide wood planks, and leaded-glass windows faced the street. An ornate door of dark wood sat beneath an overhang supported by two stone pillars.

Tower climbed the steps and knocked on the door.

A woman with gray hair piled high and wearing round spectacles answered.

"May I help you?" she asked.

"I'm here to speak with Joseph Parker," Tower said.

She hesitated, but Tower knew Parker was there. He'd watched him leave the Big River Club and amble over to the WCA just after lunch. Tower figured he was either working or napping.

"Is he expecting you?" the woman asked.

"Yes, he is," Tower said. It wasn't a lie. Parker had to know that sooner or later he, Tower, would show up.

The woman let him inside through the spacious front room that held a secretary's desk and a giant clock over which hung a set of longhorns. Windows with thick glass let natural light into the space and heavy wood beams ran the length of the ceiling.

There were several offices in the rear of the building, and the woman took Tower to the one at the very end of the hall. She knocked, then opened the double doors.

"A Mr.—"

She turned to him.

"Tower."

"A Mr. Tower is here to see you. He says you're expecting him."

A baritone voice thundered. "Let the sonofabitch in here, Dorothy."

Dorothy scurried away as Tower walked into the office. It was a sprawling room with a thick carpet over polished wood floors. A floor-to-ceiling bookshelf took up one entire wall. A massive desk dominated the center of the room, accented by a thick cloud of cigar smoke. A side table held a decanter filled with liquor.

If Bird was here, that whiskey wouldn't last long, Tower thought.

"First of all, Mr. Parker, I want to offer my sincerest condolences—"

"Oh, go to hell, preacher."

"—on your loss."

Parker gestured with the cigar. "I let you in here to tell you if you ever come near me again it'll be the last thing you ever do."

"Why the hostility?" Tower asked. "What have I done to offend you?"

Joseph Parker got to his feet. Not an easy process. Tower remembered how big the man had seemed when he'd seen him at the club after his wife's murder. But now, in a closed space, he seemed even bigger. His hands were like giant slabs of meat, and his head looked like a granite boulder. Parker's immensity was stuffed into a white shirt that struggled to contain the man's mass, paired with charcoal pants and red suspenders. The man was simply a giant, and he seemed to swallow all of the open space in the room.

"You're here to try to exonerate that dirty preacher who got what he deserved," Parker said, his voice as cold and hard as canyon rock. "And in the process, you want to rile up Big River, splash a bunch of stories everywhere about us, and drive business away. Well I've got news for you, Mr. Tower. The only thing being driven away will be you. In an undertaker's wagon if it comes to that."

The man's face was a deep crimson.

Tower smiled at him. "You gave a speech in which you encouraged people to take up arms and defend the town. What was that speech for? Why did you make it?"

For a moment, Parker seemed off-balance. He straightened further, looked at Tower, and slid open a drawer. He pulled out a long-barreled pistol.

"I'm not sure if you understood my point," he said. "Your time in Big River is over. Some of the sheep in this town have played with you and let you run your little game of investigating. Well, that's over."

He popped open the cylinder of the revolver, showed Tower that it was fully loaded, then snapped it back into place. He held the gun at his side.

"My investigation will be over when I decide it's over," Tower said. "The funny thing about searching for truth? The ones who oppose you the most are usually the ones living a lie."

Parker's face turned so red it appeared to be on fire.

"It's well known that we have a safe here. Trail bosses sometimes bring their cash for safekeeping before they pay their riders. I always wondered what would happen if someone came in and tried to rob the place." Parker smiled at Tower. "You have three seconds to leave or I will take your presence as a sign you want to rob the place. And believe me, money is something I defend with vigor."

Tower tipped his hat.

"I'll leave you alone now," Tower said. "With your money."

Fifty-Three

Bird had been surprised by Branson's answer.

Not by the name.

But by the number.

Because Branson hadn't given up one person, he'd named two.

Thomas and Andrew Conway. The lawyers.

Bird vaguely remembered Tower pointing them out to her in the crowd of men at the Big River Club after Mrs. Parker's murder. She tried to look at the different angles as to why the Conway brothers would pay Downwind Dave to kill Stanley Verhooven. Had the old miner seen something that compromised the lawyers? And were the lawyers really pulling the strings, or had someone hired them?

Questions continued to enter her mind rapidly as Bird slowed the Appaloosa and reentered the outer limits of Big River. It had been a hard ride and she'd pushed the horse in order to get back to town before nightfall to tell Tower what she'd learned.

She rode directly to the livery, and paid the man well to give her horse some extra oats and a thorough rubdown.

Bird went to the hotel, knocked on Tower's door, and tried the handle. It was unlocked so she stuck her head inside.

He wasn't there.

Bird went back to her room, splashed some water on her face, drank two glasses of whiskey, and sat on her bed. She still had some aches and pains from being tossed out the window, but her body was recovering. Her stomach felt tight, with the occasional sharp pain reminding her of what the doctor had said.

After finishing the whiskey, she stood, left the hotel, and went back out to the street. She thought about food. She hadn't eaten since breakfast. The problem was, she wasn't hungry. In fact, whenever she thought of food, her stomach actually hurt more, which killed any hunger she might have had.

It worried her a bit. Recently, her clothes felt very loose. She'd always been thin—hence the name. But now, it seemed like everything about her was becoming harder, leaner, more finely etched.

Even her anger.

She decided to head to the saloon for some whiskey to soothe her stomach. Maybe afterward she would think about food, if she felt up to it.

The Iron Spike Saloon was relatively quiet. No big herds had arrived in the past few days, and most of the cowboys had spent their wages and moved on, heading back to Texas for a new drive or hoping to hire on at a ranch.

The bartender placed a bottle and a heavy glass in front of Bird.

She looked at the glass, hefted it.

"I like this," she said.

He filled her glass. "You must be a connoisseur. We had those shipped in from St. Louis. They're not cheap, I can tell you, but whiskey just tastes better in them."

Bird sampled the amber liquid she thought of as her partner

in life, smacking her lips after she drank.

"It does just that," she said. "Most of the time, I don't use a glass."

"You should, the air mellows it."

"You learn something every day," Bird said. "Speaking of which, have you seen that preacher around here? Mike Tower is his name. You'd recognize him from the silly expression on his face, like he's always looking for someone to help. It's annoying."

The bartender laughed.

"No, ma'am, haven't seen him around. Then again, most preachers don't cavort in these premises very often."

"Cavort. I like that word." She looked at her glass. "Can you cavort with whiskey?"

"I expect if you try hard enough, you can."

"Here's to cavorting," she said, and found the bottom of her glass. She helped herself to another.

The bartender left her to tend to other customers, and Bird felt the warmth in her stomach. It was comforting. Her appetite returned.

She drank a third whiskey, put some more money on the bar, corked the bottle, and took it with her. She thought about taking the glass, too, but decided against it. What did sound like a good idea was a thick, juicy steak. The thought of it made her mouth water. She needed to find Tower, head to a restaurant, and order some food. Wash it all down with some whiskey.

Bird walked to the church, looking up at the night sky. The stars were out in full force. One thing she had to say about Wyoming: it had no shortage of stars.

She made her way to the church, looked around, and saw no one. She then walked up and down the main street and side streets, with no sign of Tower. She went back to the hotel, checked his room again, then went down to the front desk. They had seen him leave the hotel earlier on foot. That was not news to Bird, as they had told her the same thing the first time she asked.

A long drink of whiskey straight from the bottle burned Bird's throat, and she felt a cough start, but she suppressed it, then drank again.

Damn, she thought.

Where the hell was he?

She couldn't think of where else to look. Bird wondered if he had gotten some new information and went off on his own. Or maybe he'd run into trouble. Either way, Bird decided to give it some time. He would show up sooner or later.

The stairs creaked beneath her feet as she went upstairs to her room. She pushed the door open and saw the Conway brothers in her room. One was sitting on her bed, the other was standing by the chest of drawers, with his back to her, watching her in the mirror.

The brother on the bed had a shotgun pointed at her chest.

"Welcome home, Bird," he said.

Fifty-Four

Tower pondered as he walked. Parker's reaction wasn't all that surprising. Men like him, with absolute power and great wealth, are used to everyone doing exactly what they want them to do.

Apparently, the murder of his wife hadn't changed Joseph Parker's attitude.

Tower decided it was time to nose around the sheriff's office to see if they had found anything out. There had to be a whole group of men feverishly working to find Mrs. Parker's killer, but so far, Tower had seen no sign of them.

"Mr. Tower!" a panicked woman's voice called out from behind him.

He turned to see two men pulling Evelyn Egans toward the cattle yards. Before Tower could answer, they turned a corner.

He took off on foot, running to catch up to her.

The implications ran through his mind as he ran. Was this another case of mistaken identity with the woman? Or had the hate-filled people of Big River decided to award the same fate they'd given Bertram Egans to his mother?

Tower raced around the corner.

The three had disappeared.

Where had they gone?

The cattle yards spread before him as far as the eye could

see. A long, low barn ran to the left, and a corral for horses stood off to the right.

They couldn't have gone far. If they had climbed into the cattle pens, the cows would be making plenty of noise at the disturbance. All was relatively quiet.

The horse corral held only one animal and he stood still, eating from a feed bag.

That left the barn.

Tower unconsciously reached for the gun he used to wear on his right hip. But all he grabbed was air. It was one of only a few times since becoming a preacher that he really questioned the decision not to wear a pistol.

Well, he had made his choice and now he had to live with it. Tower raced toward the barn.

He crossed the distance quickly. It was close to dark now, and although he tried to study tracks in the ground he could see none in the poor light.

Tower got to the barn and hesitated before going in. The giant doors were slightly ajar and Tower could see nothing but pure darkness in the gap between them.

He wished Bird was with him.

Tower stepped back, put his shoulder into the door and pushed. He drove it forward, his legs pushing his body inward and his momentum carrying him several feet into the barn.

Evelyn Egans stood staring at him, a gun to her head.

Two men, both wearing flour sacks with holes cut out for the eyes, stood behind her, each holding one of her arms.

Tower put up his hands.

"Please," he said. "If you're after me, let her go. She's done nothing wrong."

He heard the soft rustle of fabric behind him, the subtle

scrape of a boot on dirt, and he turned to his left, instinctively bringing his hands up.

But the wood plank caught him square on the side of the head and he heard a sickening thud, realized it was his head hitting the ground.

Fifty-Five

A shotgun never failed to command Bird's respect. Mainly because if it was close enough, there was no hope for a miss. Even a trigger pulled by a spasm from a dead man could result in an explosion of death at its most bloody.

Bird, despite an inborn confidence in her ability to get a gun out and a bullet in the lawyer's brain before his mind actually registered the action, held back.

"This is just one of the many surprises we have for you tonight," the brother with the shotgun said.

"Wait, which one of you is which?" Bird asked.

"I'm Andrew," the one facing the mirror said.

"That would make me Thomas," the one on the bed said. "But you can think of me as the handsome brother."

"Is that why he's looking in the mirror?" Bird asked. "To try to figure out how he became the ugly one?"

Andrew Conway turned away from the mirror. He had a gun in his hand, and like the shotgun, it was also pointed directly at Bird.

"Actually, I'm the handsome one, and the smart one. He's stronger than me, which is why I use him to haul firewood up large hills."

The bed squeaked as the brother with the shotgun ignored

his brother and said, "First of all, we'd like you to know that we are in possession of your preacher friend."

The other brother turned back to the mirror.

"Well that doesn't sound very friendly," Bird said. "Or legal. Aren't you two supposed to be lawyers?"

"We are."

The brother facing the mirror practiced putting his gun in his waistband, taking it out quickly, then putting it back. He adjusted the butt of the gun, changing the degree to which it stuck out.

"And as a lawyer, I want you to know the importance of a verbal contract in a court of law," the other one continued. "The average citizen isn't aware of it, but a verbal contract can be just as legally binding as a written contract. Therefore, when you agree to leave Big River now, and wire us when you get to the telegraph office in Mumford, which is two hundred miles away, and agree to stay away from Big River for the rest of your life, you are in fact, entering into a verbal contract with the two of us."

"You sure are a bag of hot air," Bird said.

"And since my brother and I are both barristers, pointing this out to a judge in a court of law will land you in a great deal of trouble with a fair amount of jail time," the one by the mirror said.

"Part two of your sentence will be the untimely demise of your preacher," the other one said. "I'm afraid you will only get jail time, but he will most likely receive the death penalty."

"I see," Bird said. "And you swear all of this is true, under oath?"

The brothers hesitated.

"Miss Hitchcock, now is not the time for trite attempts at humor. I sincerely hope you understand the gravity of the situation."

The brother with the pistol pushed Bird's belongings across

the floor to her with the tip of his boot.

"Time for you to leave," he said.

"Please don't come back," the other brother said.

Bird smiled and picked up her things.

"So, you two are the big lawyers in town, is that right?" she asked.

"While an understatement, that would be true."

"Don't most lawyers have one really big client who pays most of the bills?"

The brother on the bed thumbed back both of the shotgun's hammers. The sound of them clicking into place seemed very loud to Bird.

"If there's one thing I have the utmost respect for, it's the law," Bird said.

She nodded to the brothers, although the gesture was really directed at the shotgun, and left.

Fifty-Six

He had been a soldier, a spy behind enemy lines in the Civil War, and then a private investigator. But now, Mike Tower was forced to admit that those professions seemed utterly tame compared to his time as a traveling preacher.

The lump on the side of his head would most likely agree.

He felt disoriented, as if he couldn't get his balance, and then realized that he was no longer on the ground, but riding in a wagon.

His hands and feet were tied, and he was blindfolded. He heard the horses, felt the bounce of the wagon wheels, and reached his right foot out until he hit the side of the wagon to brace himself against the jostling. Free from the constant movement, he was able to get his bearings back.

On some level, he had suspected the barn was a trap, but there had been little choice. He could have gone for help and looked for Bird, all while the two men held Evelyn Egans inside the barn. If it was a trap, they would have been doing nothing to her. On the other hand, if it wasn't a trap and if he hadn't rushed in, they would have had all the time in the world to do whatever they wanted with her.

It was foolish, but it had been the right thing to do.

Now, he had to deal with the consequences.

He stayed with his leg pressed against the side of the wagon until it began to cramp, and just when he was about to shift position, the wagon stopped.

Someone threw the wagon's tailgate down and Tower felt a hand grab his ankles. He was pulled from the wagon, dumped onto the ground, and then hoisted to his feet. Someone pushed him forward and he stumbled on the uneven ground. A heavy door opened and Tower smelled the dank interior of another barn.

The blindfold was torn from his head, and he was knocked to the ground.

He looked up at several men surrounding him, all wearing flour sacks like the two men who'd held Evelyn Egans captive. They were all armed, their guns at the ready. Common sense told Tower not to try to make an escape attempt. He wouldn't make it out the door.

The nearest hooded man held out a pair of shackles. Tower allowed himself to be restrained. Another man chained the handcuffs with a lock to an iron peg in the barn wall.

"Make yourself comfortable, it's going to be a while," one of the men said. Some of the other men laughed as they left the barn.

The group parted and two more men, also wearing flour sacks, brought in the Egans woman. They put her in shackles and chained her to the same.

Then the men left.

Evelyn Egans began to sob. Her shoulders heaved with each guttural moan and Tower knew the woman was terrified.

He tested the strength of the shackles and that of the iron peg. There was no way he could break them, they were solid and well built.

Evelyn Egans' sobs gradually subsided to soft whimpers. Outside, Tower thought he heard the wagon being moved, maybe heading back to town. He assumed they had left Big River, but he couldn't be sure. He had no idea how long he'd been in back of the wagon.

Finally, he turned to Mrs. Egans.

She looked up at him, her face a mixture of grief and shock.

"Why don't you tell me the truth?" Tower asked.

Fifty-Seven

Bird hit the trail and the bottle simultaneously. She hated being surprised, and although her first instinct was to shoot her way to a resolution, this time she decided to think things through.

There was little doubt she would be followed, so she took her time once she was past the outskirts of Big River. It was a dark night, a thick layer of clouds obscured any light from the moon and stars. Bird didn't mind. The Appaloosa was a gifted horse in the dark, able to discern trails on her own, and the ability to alert Bird at any signs of danger.

Which meant Bird was free to drink.

The bottle she'd started drinking from when she left the saloon was nearly empty. She drained the rest of it, threw the bottle into the air, waited for a hint of reflection from what little light existed, drew her gun, and fired. The bottle exploded in a shower of glass, the pieces landing silently in the dirt and grass.

Bird broke out a new bottle, a thick square vessel filled with bourbon. She had bought it at the Big River General Store when they'd first come to town, but she knew it was the cheap stuff so she'd avoided it. Now, it would have to do.

She drank. The bourbon was raw and unrefined, burning her throat as it went down. Instead of the usual warmth she felt at the start of a good drunk, this time, the heat was fiery and jagged.

Bird shifted in the saddle as a pain in her lower stomach blossomed with a bubbling intensity. She took another drink, but the pain only intensified.

Damn Mike Tower, she thought.

He'd gone and gotten himself kidnapped while she was putting Martin Branson out of his misery. Where had they gotten him? At the hotel? No, the front-desk clerk said Tower had left on his own accord earlier in the day.

Now what the hell was she going to do?

At the base of a narrow plateau, Bird halted the Appaloosa and looked back at her trail. She heard nothing, but thought she caught a glint of dull light on something metallic a long way behind her. It was too far for someone to shoot her with a rifle so she paid it no mind. Her horse's ears were pointed forward, eager to get moving and perform her duties as a trail boss. Hell, if her horse wasn't worried about what was behind them, she wouldn't worry either.

Bird drank more of the rotgut bourbon and urged the Appaloosa forward. They steadily climbed the plateau to the top, and started their descent.

This side of the wide ridge was much steeper than the one they'd just traversed. Bird's horse slowed, then jumped quickly to avoid rocks that tumbled past them, stirred by their passing.

At the bottom of the hill was a dry gully full of rocks. Bird felt her horse gather itself, and then it leapt over the opening. She braced herself, wincing as the impact came. The force of their landing seemed to drive the pain in Bird's belly deeper into her insides.

The pain exploded inside of her.

Bird held on to the saddle as the horse swung into an easy canter, as eager to get away from the plateau as she was.

Ahead of them was a broad, flat plain she recognized. They were only a quarter-mile or so from Killer's Draw.

Bird thought maybe she would stop and drink from the creek. Her throat was aching and the fire raced up her belly. Suddenly, she began to cough. Blood spurted from her mouth. The coughing continued, and she felt herself choking either on the blood or from the lack of air. Pain wrapped around her face and the world began to turn blurry and white. Bird had the sense she was floating and then her face hit something very, very hard.

White was replaced with black.

Fifty-Eight

"I'm an actress," Mrs. Egans said. "That man who accosted us in the street was right. My real name is Rose Sutton."

Tower shook his head. He should have known.

"I'm sorry. I didn't think anyone was going to get hurt. I'm just a damned actress for Christ's sake, and not a very good one."

It appeared to dawn on her that she was talking to a preacher.

"I'm sorry," she said again.

Tower had many questions but he forced himself to relax, keep his voice even.

"It's alright," he said. "I understand. Everything is going to be fine. Just let me ask you a few questions. First, who hired you?"

Rose shook her head. Her voice cracked and she started to cry. "I don't know."

Tower understood the helplessness the woman was feeling so he softened his voice. "Explain that to me," he said, trying to sound as reassuring as possible.

"I was hired through my manager back East. He wired me the instructions, told me someone would pay two hundred dollars, minus my manager's commission, of course, to act like this dead preacher's mother. So, that's what I did. They gave me a little background—enough that I could pull the part off, I guess."

"Did your manager know who was going to pay him? Did they say why they wanted you to do this?"

The woman shook her head. "I don't think so. He's too busy for that kind of thing. They probably sent in the request and he figured I was the best choice for the part so he gave it to me. I probably only got it because I'm one of the few actresses old enough to play the part of a mother."

"How long were you supposed to stay? And what were your instructions for afterward?"

"The job was for just a few days," Rose Sutton said. "I was supposed to make sure I was seen around town, gather whatever of the young man's belongings was still there, and then leave. Once I got home, which is Baltimore, I was supposed to let my manager know the acting job had been successful, and then I would be paid."

"Why were you in the land office?" Tower asked.

"That was part of the job, too," she said. "Apparently, this young man had been doing some research on land ownership and—"

The door to the barn swung open and a group of men entered. They all wore hoods with holes cut out for the eyes. Two of them went to Rose, undid her chains, and led her from the barn. She struggled against them and then looked back at Tower.

"I'm sorry," she said.

Tower just nodded at her. He prayed they wouldn't hurt her and hoped they understood she was just a pawn.

The rest of the men formed a circle around Tower. They undid his chains and then stepped back, and parted at the center.

A man stepped forward.

He was the only one not wearing a hood.

At first, Tower thought it was the man Bird had called Mr. Seven. He was a giant. Not fat like Joseph Parker, just tall and wide, but lean. Tower looked at his face. No, it wasn't Mr. Seven, but the man had to be related.

He looked at Tower, then carefully took off his shirt, folded it neatly, and handed it to the nearest man.

The group of men widened as the man closed in on Tower.

He realized what was about to happen. He was going to have to fight this giant. Tower also understood the significance of the hoods. All of the men in the group still wore theirs, which meant they thought Tower would get out of this alive.

But the man bearing down on him wore no disguise.

Which meant he had no intention of letting Tower live.

Tower shook his hands free.

"This is for my brother," the man said.

The biggest fist Tower had ever seen came at him. He ducked it and drove a short left hook into the man's midsection.

It was like hitting the side of a horse.

The man's stride hitched and Tower stepped back, lashed out with a straight left that pulverized the man's nose.

The big man swung and Tower ducked it, but the next one, he never saw coming.

Fifty-Nine

The face was ghostly white. That made sense to Bird, because it had to be a ghost.

Cold rocks jabbed into her back, and Bird shivered. Everything felt uneven to her, the ground, the sky, her mind. Various parts of her body felt numb and she wanted to stand up but spent a long moment trying to figure out which way that would be.

The face had been there, but now it was gone. In an instant. What had it looked like? Bird couldn't remember. It might have been an angel, but she didn't believe in them.

By instinct, Bird called out to her horse, and heard her answer from not too far away.

That was good, Bird thought. Death loves a person without a horse.

Pain twisted her insides and she cried out. Darkness answered and when the light returned, Bird was no longer on the rocks. She was on something soft. And there was a blanket over her.

A face appeared, but this time it was one she recognized.

It was her horse.

The Appaloosa's eye glinted in the darkness and she seemed to be willing Bird to do something.

Bird sat up, this time knowing where up was.

She looked around.

There was no one.

Had she actually seen the face? It had been a woman's face.

Something odd struck her about the memory.

Why had the face looked so familiar?

EPISODE FIVE

Sixty

Goddamn and what the hell?

Bird leaned over the pommel as her horse carried her forward. What was going on with her? For most of her life, she had always felt in control, even when an outside observer might say otherwise.

But not now.

Physically, things were unbalanced, spinning around, and her mind was following.

She leaned to the side and spit out a bloody glob. She was cold, her stomach ached, and her head hurt.

But most of all, she worried about what she may or may not have seen during the night. The face haunted her. It was ghostly, a blur of white, like a puff of smoke being carried by the wind. It had been there but was gone in an instant, barely long enough for her to register that it looked like a face.

Was she hallucinating? It wouldn't be the first time, she thought. There'd been plenty of long, drunken nights when she wasn't sure if something had actually happened or if she'd imagined it. Had the rotten whiskey and the fall from her horse caused her to have a vision? But she hadn't imagined being covered with a blanket. Had she done that herself? Or had the ghost done so? And was that related to the strange voice and the sight of a child she'd seen before at Killer's Draw?

Bird leaned back, winced in pain, and dug through her saddlebag.

Damn. She was out of whiskey.

She ground her teeth together, straightened in the saddle, and brought the Appaloosa to a stop.

What town had Conway said? Mumford? She knew it was northeast of Big River and a long, long ride. In her condition, it would take even longer. With the way she felt right now, the idea of riding over the mountains filled her with dread. She'd never make it.

There had to be a better way.

She went over a few possible scenarios, forcing her mind to work and stop thinking about how much she needed a drink.

Bird turned the Appaloosa around and headed back toward Big River. She rode for several miles before they came across a stream with pure, cold mountain water. She let her horse drink first, then knelt and drank deeply. The cold water soothed her throat so she drank more. She sat back, feeling the soothing liquid wind its way through her body.

She leaned down to the stream and drank again, then splashed some of the water on her face. It was ice cold and it revived her. Her entire body was cold, but in a good way. For some reason, the cold reenergized her and she suddenly felt like she had her bearings back.

Bird got to her feet, mounted her horse, and pushed across the stream, thinking through her options as she rode.

There was no doubt someone had followed her out of town and was now waiting for word from the telegraph operator that she had arrived in Mumford.

Anger flamed within her. Many things could set off her temper, but few could ignite this kind of slow fury—the kind that usually resulted in violence. But one of them never failed to put a razor edge on her anger.

And that was the idea of someone trying to control her.

To manipulate her.

To force her to do anything at all.

She had a simple solution for those people.

Make them pay.

Sixty-One

Tower tasted dirt and blood in his mouth and knew he had to act fast. The blow from the big man had nearly taken his head off. He wouldn't survive many more of those.

Tower rolled onto his back, then lurched to his feet, just as the man moved in on him.

Tower knew he was in trouble. He still hadn't fully recovered from the dynamite blast, and the last blow made him feel disoriented, but he figured he might have a chance. Men as large as the one before him rarely had to fight. But he, Tower, had grown up scrapping and fighting, excelling at hand-to-hand combat during the war. He knew things that he hoped the giant coming at him didn't.

The man swung at Tower, a tremendous blow with the weight of the world behind it, but it was a wide and looping punch that assumed Tower might back away. Men of this size were used to trying to hit targets that were running in the opposite direction.

So Tower took a different tack. He lunged in closer to the man and drove a right straight into his opponent's midsection, followed by a flurry of wicked blows delivered with as much strength as he could muster directly into the man's lower body.

He worked the belly, the side, and one wicked uppercut directly into the solar plexus.

The man gave up punching and threw his arms around Tower, pulling him closer. Tower felt the incredible strength as he was crushed and then lifted from his feet. The big man squeezed, putting bone-crushing pressure on Tower's spine. Tower couldn't breathe and the pain intensified by the second. He reared back and head butted the man, but the attacker's grip didn't loosen. Instead, it threw the man off balance, and they toppled over onto the ground.

Tower heard his opponent gasp as the breath was driven from his body.

Tower was faster to his feet, and as his adversary tried to stand, Tower battered his face with savage blows that split the man's lips and cut open a cheek, spraying blood.

The man made a primal growl and rushed at Tower, who sidestepped the charge and boxed him on the ear.

Tower stepped back, watching as the man turned to face him. He was breathing hard, clearly not used to being struck with such force or seeing his own blood.

Tower darted in, lashed a straight jab that flattened the man's nose, then stomped on his instep. The giant charged again, not wanting to box, but to get his monstrous arms around Tower again and finally crush him to death.

Tower began to step back but someone behind him tripped him and he landed on his back. As his opponent went to pounce on him, Tower lifted his knees, placed his boots on the man's chest, and kicked, sending the man over Tower and onto the floor behind him, producing a cloud of dust and hay.

Tower used his own momentum to flip over, landing astride the big man. He used his knees to pin the man's arms and then hammered the giant's face with blow after blow until he was brutalizing nothing but a bloody mask.

Someone pushed Tower off the beaten man. Tower got to his feet and watched as the bloodied beast struggled to stand.

When he finally did, Tower stepped in and threw a punch with everything he had, corkscrewing his body and rotating his fist for maximum drive. The blow tore directly into the man's throat, producing a loud snap that signified to everyone in the barn that the giant man's neck had been broken.

The man swayed briefly and dropped to the floor, his eyes wide with disbelief, and then death.

Sixty-Two

Bird sat on her horse outside of Big River. She had waited until dusk to make her approach and now was at the town's south end, taking advantage of a cattle herd that was holding range until a pen opened up. To a person looking her direction from town, she probably looked like a cowboy taking a break.

"What do you say we have a drink?" she asked the Appaloosa. The horse looked back at her.

"I know, you don't drink whiskey," Bird said. "Ever since that time you wound up dancing on some tables."

Bird broke out the bottle she'd just bought from a cowboy leaving town, and drank. From her vantage point, she had an excellent view of the tiny telegraph office sitting off on its own, just across from a tack shop.

Bird knew that most telegraph offices closed around this time, although they could be unique to the behavior of the operator, especially if it was a one-man operation and that operator liked to head off to the saloon in late afternoon.

Sometimes, operators lived in their offices, but that was generally in towns smaller and less affluent than Big River.

While she waited, she went over her plan. It would have to be flexible because there was no way of knowing where it would lead. Most of the scenarios depended on who the operator was and what his evening habits were.

After fewer than fifteen minutes of watching, the door to the telegraph office opened and a short, squat man exited, locking the door behind him. He wore dark pants, a white shirt with stripes, and a visor.

He walked behind the building, and much to Bird's relief, headed away from the main street of Big River, instead angling for a cluster of residential homes east of town.

Bird followed, striking a parallel path that put some buildings between them.

After a few blocks, her quarry turned down a street and approached a single-story house with a wide porch and a chimney made of river rock. He opened the door and went inside.

Bird brought the Appaloosa to a stop and assessed the block. There were wide, empty lots, a house under construction, and a section of three homes packed together on one lot, each home identical to the next.

In front of one was a little girl sitting on a swing hanging from a tree in the front yard. Luckily, she was facing the other way. Bird watched her for a moment, wondering what it was like to grow up in one town, in one house, and never be shuttled from house to house, family to family, wondering when all hell would break loose.

Bird shook the thoughts away, took another drink of whiskey, put the bottle into her saddlebag, then rode straight up to the house the telegraph operator had entered, tied up her horse, and walked in.

The telegraph operator stood at a table, his visor off, sleeves undone, a glass of whiskey in his hand. On a sideboard next to him was a crystal decanter filled with whiskey and another glass sitting on a lace doily.

"What the hell?" he asked. He set his glass of whiskey on the table, and turned to face Bird. He noted both of her guns.

Bird walked up to him and kneed him in the groin. The man dropped to his knees.

She picked up his whiskey glass and drank.

"Sorry about hitting you there, but I can't leave a mark on your face, for what I need you to do."

Bird drained the glass of its contents.

"Thanks for the drink, by the way."

Sixty-Three

Tower sat in the dark. The blackness wasn't limited to the barn, though. He realized he had killed a man. It wasn't his first, but it had been a long time since he'd ended someone's life, and he felt sick to his stomach. The adrenaline that had pumped through his body during the fight was now gone, replaced by exhaustion. The heaviness of emotion that came with killing another human being rested on his soul with suffocating oppression. It wasn't a feeling he had ever wanted to experience again and his decision to become a preacher, to leave behind the violent life he'd known as a soldier and a detective, now seemed like a cruel joke.

He tried to push those thoughts aside. The immediate danger was even greater now that he'd killed one of them. Up until then, he had hoped they might let him live. That hope was dwindling. He suspected they were somewhere trying to figure out what to do next, as he was confident their plan had not included the preacher killing their enforcer.

Tower struggled against his bindings. His wrists were tied behind him, and his feet were bound together. Whoever had done it had performed the task with thorough professionalism. His restraints were unyielding.

Just as he accepted that his only option now was to wait, the barn door swung open and three men came in.

Each of them carried some sort of club. Tower saw that one carried a piece of lumber, another brandished an axe handle.

The good news was they still wore their flour sacks.

Two of the men grabbed Tower by the arms and dragged him into the center of the barn.

The third walked up and measured the distance between himself and Tower with the axe handle.

"That was quite the job you did on Big Henry," he said.

"Thank you," Tower said.

"You think this is funny?" the one asking questions asked Tower.

"Killing someone is never funny," Tower said. "I did what I had to do."

"Where'd a preacher like you learn to fight like that?"

"I wasn't always a preacher."

"So, what, were you some kind of fighter? A boxer?"

"I was a survivor," Tower said.

"We'll see about that," one of the other men said.

"I have one question for you," the man directly in front of Tower said. "If you can answer this question, and we think you're telling the truth, you might survive this."

He pressed the axe handle against Tower's neck.

"If you lie you won't survive. Understand?"

Tower nodded as best he could.

"So, answer this question," the man said. "Where is she?"

Sixty-Four

"What's your name?" Bird asked.

"Oliver Barnes," the telegraph operator said.

The man was on his hands and knees. He had just finished vomiting onto the floor and looked like a dog who knew the punishment wasn't over.

Up close, Bird saw that he was very short and older than she had thought. Maybe close to sixty. He had close-cropped gray hair, pudgy fingers, and tiny feet. His gold-rimmed spectacles were on the floor next to him.

"Look, lady, just take whatever you want," he said. "I don't have much, and what I do have certainly isn't worth getting killed over."

Bird walked over to the sideboard and grabbed the whiskey decanter and a glass. She brought it over to the table, poured herself a drink.

"You seem like a practical man," Bird said. "Oh, where are my manners? Can I get you a drink, too?" she asked.

Barnes shook his head. "I don't think I could handle it right now."

"Good point," Bird said. She looked at the whiskey in her glass. "Okay, I have to ask. Is this the good stuff? Because I've recently found the rotgut gives me some major problems."

"It's excellent whiskey."

Bird tasted the liquor and agreed. She looked around, noted that although the room was sparsely furnished, each high-quality piece was well taken care of. She pulled out one of her guns and set it on the smooth, polished surface of the table.

"Oh God," Barnes said.

"Don't worry, I'm not going to kill you right now. However, I have killed many, many men. You, however, have a good chance of surviving if you follow my instructions carefully."

Barnes nodded.

"First, a few questions," she said. "How long have you been in charge of the telegraph office here in Big River?"

"I was the one who set it up here, years ago, and no one else has been involved."

"That's good to know. Now, do you know Thomas and Andrew Conway?"

"Of course I do. They're some of my most frequent customers."

"Do you know them personally? Are you friends, or just business associates?"

"Business associates," Barnes said.

"Did they tell you anything about watching for a telegraph from one of their friends in Mumford?"

Barnes furrowed his brow. "I believe Andrew did, but he said it wouldn't be here for a little while. Why?"

"Well, it just arrived."

"It did?"

"Yes, it did. And tomorrow morning, bright and early, you are going to send word to the Conways that the telegraph arrived and that Bird Hitchcock is alive and well in Mumford, having gotten there well ahead of schedule."

"I understand."

"Now, what are the chances you won't do as I've instructed?"

"I will do it."

"I believe you. However, a lot of men don't like being given orders by a woman."

"I have no issue with that."

"Some men would wait until I'm gone and then start to feel like no woman has the right to tell them what to do. They need to feel big in the britches so they don't do as I say."

Barnes nodded. "You're Bird Hitchcock. I'll do as you say."

"I appreciate that, but I've decided to give myself a little bit of insurance," Bird said. "While you were revisiting your lunch, I found some correspondence in your desk with a woman named . . ."

Bird took out a slip of paper from her pocket and read.

". . . Lily Barnes."

Barnes lowered his head and his shoulders sagged.

"Your sister or your mother?"

"Sister. She's my sister."

"Here is my proposition. You do as I've instructed, and everything will be just fine between us. I'm projecting my stay here in Big River to be over quite soon, so once I'm gone your life can return to normal and no one will be the wiser."

Bird lifted her gun from the table, and held it casually against her leg.

"However, if you betray our little agreement here, I will hunt you down and blow your brains out all over the floor, and then I will ride to . . ."

Bird again pulled the letter from her pocket.

". . . 213 Jaybird Lane, Denver, Colorado, and shoot your sister in the ankles, knees, and elbows before putting one directly between her eyes. I will then repeat the process with every single human being living at that address. However, before I shoot her, I will explain that you, Oliver, had a chance to save her life but instead did something very, very stupid. That way, in addition to dying a horrible death, she will die with the very final thought of her life being that her brother failed her."

Bird got to her feet.

"Do you understand?"

"I understand," Barnes said.

Bird grabbed the decanter of whiskey on her way out.

Sixty-Five

Tower looked at the man facing him with an axe handle. He looked hard at the eyes, partially hidden behind the flour sack. Did he recognize the eyes?

"Where is *she*?" Tower repeated. "Are you talking about Bird? How would I know where she is?"

Tower heard the blow before he felt it. One of the men behind him had cracked him in the ribs. The blow rocked him and he toppled over, his face pressed into the floor of the barn. He had felt something give in his side, and it was hard to breathe. The pain showed no sign of going away.

"Not that saddle tramp," the man in front of him said, his voice slightly muffled by the sack. "We know where she is. We want to know about the other one, the one that son-of-a-bitch reporter was following."

Tower's mind immediately went back to the papers that Martha Jeffire had given him before she left Big River. There had been an article about a prostitute, and a transcript of Joseph Parker's speech, without any context.

"I don't know what you're talking about," Tower said.

The men converged then clubbed, kicked, and punched him, cursing him as a liar and a thief. Tower tried to shield himself from the blows but there were too many coming from all directions. They worked him over, the worst of it being when someone stomped on his left hand. He had stopped feeling anything long before they were done, witnessing the beating as if he were an uninvolved bystander.

When they did stop, all he could hear was their heavy breathing from the exertion.

He tasted blood and hoped that the bleeding was from a cut in his mouth and that nothing had been punctured internally.

"Try again," one of them finally said.

Tower tried to think but his brain wasn't working right and an insistent throbbing came from every inch of his body. What could he tell them?

Suddenly, an idea came to him.

"Harlan's Crossing," he said. "That's where she is."

The barn fell silent, and Tower knew they had been half expecting him to provide no information whatsoever. His intuition told him that his answer had caught them off guard.

Harlan's Crossing was the town Martha Jeffire had told them her husband had gone to in search of Bertram Egans' love interest. That had all been a fiction. But when someone doesn't believe the truth, you may as well go with a lie.

"Where in Harlan's Crossing?" the leader of the group asked dubiously.

"I don't know. Jeffire's information was vague," Tower gasped. Every time he spoke, the pain in his side stabbed at him. "All I know is that's where he thought she was, so I was going there tonight to investigate."

The men whispered among themselves, and Tower couldn't help but wonder if his fate was being decided right here, right now, in this barn.

They formed a tighter circle around him.

"Say good night, Mr. Tower."

The sound of wood on flesh filled the air inside the barn.

Sixty-Six

The morning sun lit up the section of walk just outside a tack shop, but it provided little warmth.

Bird sat in a chair, tipped back against the wall, with a hat over her eyes. She had a tin coffee cup in her hand but it didn't hold coffee. Inside was the last of the telegraph operator's whiskey. She sipped it, silently thanking Oliver Barnes for having such high standards.

It would have been easy for her to get a fresh bottle in a saloon, but undoubtedly someone would recognize her. For now, she was determined to make this last. And she might have to wait awhile.

It occurred to her that she hadn't covered whether Oliver Barnes should go to the Conways first thing in the morning and give them the artificial news or whether he should wait until they came to him. She had been so intent on scaring the living hell out of him that she missed that detail.

In any event, it probably didn't matter. If Barnes went to the Conways, it would look like he realized how important the job was that they had tasked him with. If he waited, it would appear relatively normal.

Bird sipped from the cup.

She supposed it work either way. For Tower's sake, she hoped so.

She suddenly realized that she missed him.

The thought blossomed in her mind before she could tamp it down. She shook her head. She didn't *miss* him. That was such a strong word, clearly not the right choice for what she was thinking. She was *concerned* about him. That was more accurate. And she had every right to worry. These bastards didn't seem to care too much one way or the other about killing people, and although she knew Tower was a lot tougher than he looked, they didn't know that. Maybe that would give him a fighting chance.

Bird was surprised to see one of the Conway brothers cross the street and enter the telegraph office. She wondered if he was going there to check specifically on her supposed progress to Mumford or if he was on other business. At least she could be certain he would get the message.

She waited, wondering whether Oliver Barnes was sufficiently terrified to keep his word or whether he was telling Conway right now that Bird Hitchcock was back in town. Bird figured she would watch the manner in which Conway left the building, looking for any signs that he was now the hunted.

Down the street, a door slammed and a cowboy trotted past, adjusting his lariat on the way to the cattle yards. In the distance, she heard the train engine start to chug as it made its departure from Big River.

Conway emerged from the telegraph office walking more quickly than he had on the way over. Bird watched him disappear around the corner and noted that he made no attempt to look for a watcher. That might mean something, it might not. She gulped the rest of the whiskey, set the cup down, and stood up from the chair. She strolled down to the end of the street, then leaned up against the corner of the building, rounding it as if she just wanted to get out of the sun.

As she suspected, and had hoped, Conway wasn't going back to his office. As she watched, he went into a saloon, which instantly filled Bird with envy. She would have to find a way to get some whiskey for the ride ahead.

Bird watched and waited until Conway emerged with another man who immediately jumped on a horse and rode away. The Conway brother turned and headed back in the general direction of his office, seemingly unconcerned about whether he was being watched. She was fairly confident that Barnes had done his job.

Bird ducked back around the building, ran to the Appaloosa, and took off after the man.

Sixty-Seven

Tower found himself in the wagon again, surrounded by blackness. All he saw was darkness, and he hadn't been blindfolded, which Tower assumed meant that both of his eyes were now swollen shut.

Tower felt no pain. He just felt cold and outside of himself, like a spectator watching a broken man being unceremoniously tossed around inside a buckboard as he slid around on its surface, knowing full well that he was sliding on his own blood.

When the wagon stopped, he braced himself, knowing what was about to come. The sound of voices, a horse snorting, and then the liftgate being thrown open.

Tower was pulled from the wagon and dumped on the ground. He managed to crack one eye open enough to let in a slit of light. He saw the legs of three men once again surrounding him.

Nothing hurt anymore. He heard the men talking softly, and his eye closed again, returning him to darkness. Something was wrong with his hearing, because he could only catch bits and pieces of the conversation going on above him.

"—not taking him way over there!"

"This is far enough."

"Just dump him, right?"

Tower heard the horses stamp their feet, and then hands grabbed him. Something sharp jabbed him in the side, the pain cutting through the fog of his mind. His brain just recognized that it was probably another wound but at this point, they weren't worth keeping track.

The hands lifted him and for a moment, he wondered if they were going to put him back into the wagon. But he felt himself being swung back and forth, like he was in the middle of a tug-of-war. And then the hands were no longer on him and he was airborne.

"You've been Rectified!" one of the men yelled.

Tower hung in the air for only a moment as he landed and then he was rolling over and over. Something smashed into his face and he floated high above himself, fading into a gauzy shadow until ice cold enveloped him. He was pushed back out of the cold before it washed over him again, one final time.

Sixty-Eight

Despite the flat landscape through which Conway's messenger rode, Bird had no trouble following him undetected. There was no attempt to cover tracks and she employed the simple tactic of waiting until the rider nearly disappeared from the horizon before moving forward.

Bird quickly realized that they were moving in the general direction of the Parker spread, although sometimes in this country it was difficult to know where one man's property ended and another's began. She had heard in some places they were starting to fence the open ranges, but that hadn't gotten to Wyoming yet. Bird was pretty sure there would be hell to pay if someone tried to do that out here.

Morning passed to afternoon and then the rider finally broke from the trail and headed over several passes before coming to a cluster of outbuildings. Bird could see no main house, however, nor were there any cattle in sight. If she was on Parker's extended range, she saw no sign of it.

Bird rode closer to the group of buildings and saw a few other horses but no other signs of life. A buckboard stood off to the side, horses still hitched.

She backed down the hill she was on, then circled around and found a coppice through which she could see the building into which Conway's rider had disappeared. Bird stationed herself behind the trees, barely able to see the scene below, which meant they would have trouble seeing her. As if she understood they were in for a wait, the Appaloosa began to munch grass.

The horse had nearly gotten its fill when a group of men emerged from the biggest building and went to their horses. Two of them walked to the wagon and climbed up onto the bench. She couldn't tell if there was anything or anyone in the back of the wagon and hadn't yet seen any sign of Tower.

The entire group left together, reversing the rider's original path. Bird figured they were returning to Big River.

She waited, giving them plenty of time, and then followed to see if they had gone back to the main trail.

They had.

Once satisfied they wouldn't be circling back, Bird returned to where the outbuildings sat. It was the perfect place to hold someone captive. With the exception of the larger barn, most of the buildings looked like overgrown line shacks, temporary quarters for cowboys in search of lost cattle during the winter.

She carefully approached the buildings, alert to any signs of activity, but all was still.

Skipping smaller buildings that appeared uninhabited, she went straight for the barn. Bird removed the simple wood plank that held the door in place and then pulled the door open.

The barn was empty.

Bird walked into the center of the barn, noticed some loose hay that had been pushed around, and saw clearly defined pools of dried blood. She squatted on her heels to take a closer look.

She he had no way to tell if it was animal or human blood. But she doubted someone suddenly decided to butcher a cow in the middle of the barn.

Bird left, shut the door behind her, and walked to where the wagon had been.

When the men had left, they'd continued in a circle around the barn and back to the trail. Bird followed the wagon's previous trail, which showed that it had come in at a tangent from the main path.

She could tell the load in the trailer hadn't been too substantial because the wheel ruts were superficially deep at best. But there had been enough weight to make the trail easy to follow. She set out after the group, convinced that Tower was in the back of the wagon. Unless it was six feet under the prairie somewhere, in an unmarked grave, there was no other place for him to be.

It was early evening by the time the wagon's tracks led her to a rise in the trail that ended at a washout. A river raced below her, forceful and frothy.

She could see that the wagon had stopped, then turned to the right and moved on.

The Appaloosa had no desire to walk to the ledge, so Bird dismounted and walked there. Dirt and rocks cascaded sharply into a swollen river.

At the edge of the water was a body.

Sixty-Nine

He had a pulse, but it was weak.

Bird looked at Tower's face. It was a devastating mess of cuts and bruises, swollen, puffy eyes, black circles, and smears of blood. His lips were cracked, his nose was twice its normal size, and a deep gash tore across his forehead.

The rest of him wasn't much better.

The river had pushed him to the side, with only his feet submerged. Bird thought it was a miracle that he hadn't been swept away. She pulled him from the water, sure that she was aggravating his injuries, but knowing she must move him to safety.

His skin was ice cold.

She thought quickly. She could try to get him back to the barn where they'd held him, but in his current condition he wouldn't last that long. The same problem applied to getting him back to Big River. The only other town she could think of was Harlan's Crossing, which was still a long ride. And one thing she was sure of, Tower wouldn't survive a long ride. Hell, he probably wouldn't last through a short one.

That settled it. She had to warm him up here, and fast.

Bird lifted him as best she could, his feet dragging on the ground, and brought him to a dry spot above the waterline. She laid him down, got her bedroll, and covered him with it. She then climbed up onto the Appaloosa and rode hard along the riverbank, scanning both sides for what she needed.

Less than a quarter mile upriver, she found it.

A cutout just below the ledge, with enough stones and brush nearby to create a heat reflector, but far enough from the river to remain high and dry.

Bird rode back, managed to drag Tower up onto the Appaloosa, then rode quickly to the cutout and placed him on a blanket inside. She took off most of his wet clothes, then covered him again with her bedroll. Bird quickly started a fire, glad that the overhang would contain some of the smoke and hide the sight of flames from almost anyone riding by.

Next, she shored up the front of the shelter and the sides with more branches, stones, and a particularly thick branch with an abundance of foliage.

By the time she was done, not only was the temporary shelter virtually invisible from all directions but the heat from the fire inside the shelter was also bouncing back at them, warming them considerably. Whenever she detected a draft, she filled the gap with more rocks or in one case, a chunk of sod.

Bird dug through her saddlebag and found an empty bottle of whiskey. She took it down to the river, and filled it with cold water.

She gave a little to Tower, who instinctively drank. His eyes were swollen shut and it sounded like he was trying to form words.

"Go to sleep," Bird said. "We'll have plenty to talk about when you wake up."

She got the bottle of whiskey she'd bought from the cowboy back in Big River, took a drink herself, then gave some to Tower. Bird gave him more until she was sure the alcohol would help warm him on the inside.

Inside the shelter it was very warm, but there was barely room for both of them. She slipped out and made sure the Appaloosa had grass and access to the stream for water. She brought her saddlebags into the shelter and set them down next to Tower.

Bird rummaged through her bags, locating some hardtack, a few strips of dried beef, and a nearly empty bag of coffee. In the morning, she would make do with what she could. Maybe she would take her rifle and look for small game.

Bird then left to scout for dried wood, dragging as much as she could to the shelter and leaving it just outside the entrance. It was getting cold and she would have to feed the fire period-ically overnight. Plus, she wanted to hang up what was left of Tower's clothes to dry.

They were well above the waterline. In fact, the ground was perfectly dry and she wasn't worried even if it decided to rain.

She looked again at Tower.

Goddamn, she thought. They really gave him a beating, didn't they? She had to admire his toughness. He hadn't given in to the evil in the world, he was still fighting.

She guessed they had that in common.

Bird stretched out next to Tower, taking a corner of the bedroll and covering herself with it. She propped her head on the saddlebags as a pillow, and pulled the bottle next to her.

She took a long drink and closed her eyes.

Seventy

He was underwater, able to see the light above and sensing the nothingness below. He pushed to the surface but something snagged his back just as he was about to break the surface and he thrashed, worked his body back and forth, struggled to free himself to get to the surface, to the air, to light, to life—

"Tower."

He opened his eyes. Bird Hitchcock was above him, a half smile on her face.

"You snore like a grizzly bear," she said. "Might want to have a doctor look into that."

Tower turned his head and saw that he was in some kind of half cave but that he could see blue sky between piles of branches and wood. A campfire gave off heat, and he smelled something cooking.

"Rabbit for breakfast, Mr. Tower, along with some hardtack and water," Bird said. "I'd give you some of my whiskey but I'm not in the mood for sharing, seeing as how you've caused so many problems for me."

He tried to sit up, but the pain in his side stopped him. A couple of ribs were probably broken, and his left hand throbbed. At least he could see.

"You want to sit up?" Bird asked. "I recommend against it, but I'm not your boss."

"Let me try," he said. Bird held out her hand and Tower took it. He pulled himself up, gasping as the pain in his side exploded in sharp, jagged bursts. Bird went behind him, used her saddlebags and bedroll to prop him up.

"How's that?" she asked.

He nodded, gritting his teeth. "Better."

She chuckled. "You are a sight, Mr. Tower. It looks like you tried to stop a buffalo stampede with your face."

"Where are we?" he asked.

Bird took the cast-iron pan off the fire, placed a slab of wood on Tower's lap, and put the pan on top. She handed him a fork.

"You're probably not hungry, but I recommend you eat something," She squatted on her haunches and looked at Tower. "But to answer your question, we are in the middle of goddamn nowhere, near some son-of-a-bitch river where you decided to go for a swim."

"I see," Tower said.

"We need to ride to Harlan's Crossing, get you fixed up a little bit, and recover before we can do anything else. Things are going to be mighty interesting for us when we get back to Big River."

Tower alternated between nausea and ravenous hunger.

He looked at the food, at the shelter, then at Bird.

"Thank you," he said.

"Saving your hide is my job," Bird said. "And you keep me busy, that is for damn certain."

He laughed, despite himself, then winced in pain.

"So what the hell happened to you?" Bird asked. "I can

guess most of it, but I'd like to hear exactly how it came about."

Tower filled her in on his meeting with Parker, then about seeing Evelyn Egans, a.k.a. Rose Sutton, being dragged away by two men, his attempted rescue, and subsequent capture.

Bird shook her head. "Typical. Too busy trying to help someone to notice a trap. So, what happened to her?"

Tower ate a bite of roasted rabbit meat, finished the hardtack, and drank water from the whiskey bottle.

"I don't know. I suspect they let her go, but that's just a guess."

He finished the rabbit, then looked at Bird. "Look at me, I didn't even ask if you wanted some."

She shook her head. "No, I've had breakfast." She held up the whiskey bottle.

Overhead, a buzzard flew by, caught wind of the smoke, and then kept soaring along the river's edge.

"They kept asking me where *she* was," Tower said. "They were determined to get an answer out of me. So, I gave them one."

"She? Meaning me?"

Tower set the pan down next to him and drank more water.

He shook his head. "No, they didn't mean you. That's what I thought at first, but they said no. Someone else."

"Who?"

"I've got a couple of ideas."

Seventy-One

Despite the pain, Tower was able to hoist himself onto the Appaloosa, with only a tiny bit of assistance from Bird, who swung on behind him and got the horse going at a half-canter, which ate up the miles yet provided an easy rhythm to keep the pounding to a minimum for Tower.

As they rode, Bird looked for signs of people but saw no one. She figured the men who had tortured and dumped Tower would be headed for Harlan's Crossing, based on the false information Tower told her he'd given them. They had a good head start on them, but that was okay. Bird hoped they would quickly discover that Tower's information was invalid, and that they would have come and gone by the time she and Tower finally made it to Harlan's Crossing themselves.

They actually reached the small town by noon, sooner than she had figured, and Bird took great care in skirting the town before choosing a spot to enter. Having been there before helped her approach the hotel from the rear. She left Tower on the Appaloosa, then walked around to the front of the hotel.

It was mostly empty, save for a clerk at the front desk and an ancient woman sweeping the lobby. Bird paid for a room, then went back out onto the street.

Unlike the booming Big River, Harlan's Crossing survived

mostly from overflow traffic from the bigger, neighboring town. Still, a few people milled about. She looked for anyone who appeared to be watching the hotel, but they appeared preoccupied with whatever they were doing. Bird glanced across the street, scanning windows for flashes of movement, but saw nothing.

As yet, she saw no sign of a group of men from Big River, so she brought Tower around to the front, and straight up to their room on the second floor. A first-floor room had been offered, but she didn't like it for defensive purposes, which meant Tower had to climb the stairs. He succeeded at the chore, but sweat broke out along his brow and his face returned to the pale shade he'd been wearing when she'd found him by the side of the river.

In the room, she got him into bed, then gave him a loaded pistol, which he laid by his side. Bird filled the empty whiskey bottle from the water pitcher by the door, and placed it next to Tower.

She dug out her own bottle of whiskey, sat down, and looked at Tower while she took a long drink.

"Try not to get into any trouble while I try to find you a doc," she said. "Knowing you, you'll probably ignore that order."

Bird was relieved to have Tower in a proper bed. Now, she could concentrate on finding out who was responsible, not just for the state Tower was in but for the entire situation.

"I can't make any promises," Tower said. And then he smiled.

Bird was surprised to find that she liked the sight of it.

Seventy-Two

The whiskey bottle on the table next to his bed took on new meaning for Tower. In the war, the doctors had repeatedly used morphine for pain. Now, he didn't have anything. The only thing he could think of to dull the pain was the bottle Bird had thoughtfully left for him.

He popped the cork and took a long drink. He winced as it burned his throat. He didn't see how she could drink so much, and all the time. The idea of pouring this down his throat in the morning made him feel sick.

He leaned his head back onto the pillow, the bottle of whiskey in his left hand, which was still swollen and tender but didn't seem to be permanently damaged, and the gun in his right. He lifted the gun and took a good look at it. A Colt .45, impeccably cleaned and oiled, every bullet in the chamber. Some cowboys liked to keep one chamber empty, the one the hammer rests against, in case they hit a particularly hard jolt riding and the round goes off. But Bird, as in everything else she did, preferred to override caution in favor of more firepower. Tower couldn't blame her; she'd survived plenty with that strategy.

He put the pistol back down and drank again from the bottle. It was working, the pain was subsiding and a pleasant blanket of fuzziness descended on his brain and his body.

Tower closed his eyes, saw the big man in the barn coming at him, and felt the whacking of the wood planks on his body. The axe handle that had been jammed up against his throat. He wondered about Evelyn Egans, or, actually, Rose Sutton. He prayed that they let her go. Too many people had been killed already. Besides, why wouldn't they release her? She had nothing to offer them, just an actress playing a part.

His thoughts returned to the men who had beaten him and the flour sacks they wore. Something about them tugged at his memory. They were nothing new in terms of disguises. Lynch mobs were known to use them. As were vigilante groups.

Tower's eyes snapped open. Hadn't he seen a vigilante poster at the train station? When he had waited there with Morrison for Mrs. Egans' arrival?

Something else clicked in Tower's mind. He tried to sit up, but the pain forced him back into bed. He drank again from the whiskey bottle.

He remembered the men driving him out to where they'd dumped him. He recalled being pulled from the wagon, lifted into the air, swung back and forth, and then thrown off a ledge into the water below.

But they had yelled something, at least one of them had.

What had it been?

His brain had been numb with pain from the beating and the loss of blood.

He thought he'd been in and out of consciousness during the time, but he could have sworn that one of them men had yelled—

Rectified.

That's what the man had yelled.

Something about being rectified.

Vigilantes. Wearing masks. The poster at the train station.

The Rectifiers?

Seventy-Three

The Harlan's Crossing general store was in the same place it had been when she'd first come here looking for Bertram Egans' phantom girlfriend. Bird had seen virtually no one on the walk over from the hotel. Now, she entered the store, spotted the proprietor, and approached him.

"This town have a decent doctor?" Bird asked. Her eyes immediately found the row of whiskey bottles behind the counter.

"That depends. What's ailing you?" The store's owner looked like a former rancher. He had on the apron of a store clerk, but his broad shoulders and weathered hands spoke of a life lived in the open.

"Well, right now I'm thirsty," Bird said. She pointed at one of the bottles, which the owner retrieved. Bird paid, opened the bottle, and took a long drink, feeling the man's eyes upon her.

"You don't need a doctor for that. You need a bartender," he said.

"Aren't they the same thing?"

Bird took another swallow.

"No, I need a doctor for someone else, not for me," she said. "Cowboy I ride with got himself thrown from a horse. Probably broke a few ribs, among other things."

"Where is he?"

"In the hotel. I left some whiskey with him. That's the best medicine." She threw back another drink.

"Well, the way you're taking that medicine you must be awfully ill," he said.

"Not at all, sir. This whiskey is preventive medicine. Soon as I stop I get sick."

The owner nodded.

"Harlan's Crossing isn't big enough to merit a doc," he said. "But I've learned a thing or two over the years about patching up cowboys so I can probably help your friend."

"I would very much appreciate it, sir," Bird said. She was eyeing another bottle on the shelf. "And I'll take a bottle of your best, most expensive whiskey. The other stuff isn't good for you."

The store owner handed Bird a bottle, then called out. "Jimmy!"

A young boy emerged from a stockroom at the rear of the store.

"Mind the store," the owner said. "I've got to wrap up a cowboy's ribs." He turned to Bird.

"Thank you kindly," Bird said. "What's your name by the way?"

"Theodore Putti," the man said. "Call me Theo."

"And you can call me Bird."

Putti removed his apron and handed it to the young man at the counter. He walked over to a shelf, and began picking supplies and putting them into a leather case.

When he was done, he turned to Bird.

"Okay, let's see a cowboy about some ribs."

Seventy-Four

Bird knocked on the door, recalled the last time she'd entered a hotel room only to find the Conway brothers with a nice surprise for her, and pulled her gun from its holster.

"Come in," Tower said from the other side of the door.

Bird nudged the door open with her boot and peeked around the corner. Tower sat in bed, the gun in his hand pointing directly at her.

"That's better," she said. "See, you'll get captured a lot less if you always have a gun in your hand."

She stepped aside and let a visibly nervous Putti into the room, then shut the door.

"Mr. Theodore Putti, man of many trades," Bird said. "Meet Cowboy Mike, thrown from a horse last night, probably because he was half drunk to begin with."

"Pleased to meet you, Mr. Putti," Tower said. He started to sit up, winced, then fell back against the pillows.

"What the lady is trying to tell you," Putti said. "Is that I own the general store but am occasionally pressed into service for medical assistance. I don't claim to be a doctor, but I can usually handle something simple. A long time ago, I was a trail boss and had plenty of practice tending to injuries."

"I appreciate it," Tower said. "It's mostly my ribs that hurt."

"Did this horse kick you in the face, too?" Putti asked. He looked first at Tower, then back at Bird.

"It always looks that way, doc," Bird said. "It has since birth."

She crossed the room to Tower's side and pulled the bottle of whiskey from his hand. She looked at how much had been consumed since she'd left. She nodded at Tower with respect, as if she was impressed.

"Looks like I'm making progress with you," she said.

"Do you want to stay for this?" Putti said to Bird.

"What the hell, I think I'll stay." She leaned against a table holding a washbasin, and drank from the bottle. "I always love a good show."

Putti went to Tower and together they managed to remove his shirt. Bird saw the pale skin of Tower's back, inlaid with a wide swath of deep bruising and a variety of cuts.

"Jesus Christ," Bird said. "That's going to take a long time to heal."

Putti rubbed some ointment on a cloth and dabbed the open wounds on Tower's back. He did the same with some of the cuts on Tower's face. He then wrapped long strips of white cloth around Tower's body, pinning them together at the front.

"She's right," Putti said. "You definitely have a broken rib or two, but they don't appear to be horribly damaged, no bones poking through the skin, so I think they've stayed in place. And that's the important thing. It's when they break loose and start cutting up your insides that the real trouble starts. From what I can tell, you aren't bleeding inside. Just keep these around your ribs for as long as you can and gradually they'll heal. It'll take at least a month or two. There's no way to hurry it along."

Tower got his shirt back on and leaned against the pillow. Bird brought the bottle of whiskey over to him and he took a drink as Putti began gathering the items he'd brought.

"How long have you lived here in Harlan's Crossing, Mr. Putti?" Tower asked.

"Oh, I suppose it's been about ten years."

"Ever hear of a vigilante group called The Rectifiers?"

Bird looked at Tower, wondering where this line of questioning was going.

"Sure have. Everyone has around these parts," Putti said.

"Who are they?"

"Well, no one knows for sure. But they cleaned this area up a few years back. They'd finally had enough of rustlers operating around the big herds near Big River, so they put a stop to it. And then some."

"What do you mean by 'and then some'?"

Putti held up his hands. "Just rumors."

"What kind of rumors?" Bird asked.

"Look, I don't want to say anything against them, they did a lot of good for this area, it's just . . ." His voice trailed off as he searched for the right words.

"They just what?" Tower asked.

"Word was they took no prisoners, which is true for any vigilante group of course, for the most part. But some folks thought they didn't work too hard to discriminate between the guilty and the innocent."

"Sounds like every vigilante I ever knew," Bird said. She looked at Tower and noticed that he was watching Putti intently.

"What happened to them?"

"No one really knows. Their last roundup got a lot of attention because they shot a couple of rustlers, one of them a woman, and then no one ever heard from them again. But they didn't need to go out and do any enforcement. Their reputation was known all over this part of the country. No cattle thief wanted to come within a hundred miles of Big River after that one."

"So, did they operate mostly around Big River?" Tower asked.

Putti nodded.

"Yes, sir. They even had a place named after them. All those people they killed? They dumped their bodies in the same place."

He went to the door and opened it, turned back to Bird and Tower.

"Came to be known as Killer's Draw."

Seventy-Five

Bird and Tower decided to hole up at the hotel long enough for the preacher's ribs to begin to heal and the bruises on his face to fade. They couldn't go anywhere without attracting attention the way he looked now.

In the mornings, Bird would get the supplies they needed, then return to the hotel. Tower had begun to get up and pace back and forth, as much as his ribs would allow it.

Most of the time he was thinking.

About what the store owner had told him. About the papers Jeffire's widow had given him. About Killer's Draw.

He had returned Bird's whiskey to her as the pain was now relatively mild compared to those first few days. The absence of alcohol made his mind clearer, sharper.

But something danced just around the periphery of his intellect that he couldn't wrangle into a cohesive thought.

He needed just one final bit of information.

Tower returned to the bed, sat on the edge, and then swung his feet up. The pain had dulled.

Tower thought about the people he'd met in Big River. Mrs. Wolfe. Morrison. Chesser. Parker. The Conway brothers. Martin Branson.

As a group, they left a lot to be desired—

And then the pieces came together so firmly that his body jolted. He got to his feet, walked as quickly as he could to Bird's room, knocked, and went in.

She was on the bed cleaning her gun and looked up at Tower's entrance. The other gun was loaded and in her left hand, pointed at Tower's chest.

"This better be important," she said.

Tower looked at her.

"I know who killed Bertram Egans, and you're not going to believe it."

EPISODE SIX

Seventy-Six

Tower closed his eyes.

There were just too many thoughts, too many angles, to what may or may not have happened to keep organized.

When he opened his eyes, he saw Bird looking at him.

"That's some serious thinking you're doing," she said. She hefted a bottle of whiskey, and he watched with morbid fascination as her throat pulsated with the effort of imbibing.

The woman could drink; no doubt about that.

His mind went back to the papers that Roger Jeffire had given him. He wished he still had them, and that he could remember the name of the prostitute mentioned in the article. There was something about that name that wouldn't leave him alone. It was tormenting him.

"What are you thinking about, specifically?" Bird asked. "And how much longer are we going to stay in this place?"

She gestured vaguely around the room, but he knew she meant Harlan's Crossing. Bird was anxious to get back to Big River and finish things once and for all.

"I'm thinking Roger Jeffire had a good idea what happened, and I wish we had gotten more of the story. But it's too late now."

"Too late for him, too," Bird said. "Well, I'm packed and loaded, ready to go."

"I'm not," Tower said. He was still in pain from the damage to his ribs, and even simple tasks like gathering his meager belongings took three times longer than normal. The good thing was, the pain had lessened somewhat and when he had looked in the mirror this morning, the bruising was much less noticeable. Not that he cared too much about how he looked. But he had a feeling things were going to happen fast, and he wanted his body to be able to respond.

"Maybe it's not too late for Jeffire," he said.

"What the hell is that supposed to mean?" Bird asked. "He's dead."

"I mean that if we can take what he had started, we might be able to finish the story for him, by finding out, finally, what really happened."

"Tell me again what you read in that newspaper story," Bird said. She drank more whiskey and cocked her head at Tower.

"The article was about a prostitute in Baltimore who had been arrested for running a brothel and that she had been put in jail. And then there was a second article that said she disappeared. I can't remember if she escaped, or was released. In any event, it made it sound like she was long gone. As in, good riddance."

Bird considered for a moment. "So, obviously, Jeffire figured she came to Big River," she said. "Maybe set up a new brothel out here. The town has been booming with cattle and cowboys for years. Perfect place to peddle some flesh. I wonder if she changed her name. Those ladies have as many names as they do tricks in the bedroom."

Tower nodded.

"I wasn't sure if the article had anything to do, necessarily, with Bertram Egans' murder. After all, the papers were separate, and Jeffire didn't tell me anything. But when our friend here, Mr. Putti, mentioned a woman, well, it just made me think."

Bird leaned back in the chair and rested her head against the wall.

"Let me put this all together," she said. "So our prostitute gets into trouble with the law in Baltimore and heads west. She lands in Big River, sets up a brothel, and promptly runs afoul of this vigilante group, the Rectifiers, that our friend just told us about."

"No way to prove it," Tower said. "But as far as theories go, it makes a certain kind of sense."

"The woman," Bird said. "Putti said one of the last people executed by these vigilantes was a woman. Supposedly, they said she was a cattle thief. But maybe she wasn't a cattle thief at all. Maybe she was a prostitute they were running out of town."

Tower began putting his things into his bag, the bible going in last. "Maybe. But we're assuming this woman continued being a madam. But I know a lot of women who plied their trade back East, come out here to do the same thing and quickly find a lonely cowboy who wants to make an honest woman out of her. They get married and start a ranch. Not as likely, but I could see it happening."

"That doesn't make sense, though," Bird said. "The Rectifiers killed her because she started a ranch?"

"I don't know. It sounds like the Rectifiers didn't always need a good reason to take the law into their own hands."

"Which brings us back to Bertram Egans." Bird leaned forward, uncorked the bottle, and drank.

"I can't prove Jeffire thought the two were linked. I'm just guessing."

"I'd like to catch one of these Rectifiers," Bird said. "Most vigilantes I've known are cowards. The men who stand up in church and sing the loudest."

She looked at Tower. "Don't mean to insult the church."

Tower smiled. "No, I know what you mean. No shortage of folks who love to come and pray for forgiveness then run right out and do whatever they damn well please."

"Well, according to Putti, the Rectifiers operated mostly out of Big River," Tower continued. "And we both know that nothing happens in Big River without the approval of one Joseph Parker."

Bird nodded. "I'll grant you that. But that just creates a hell of a lot more questions. Like if the Rectifiers are somehow behind all of this, and the bodies at Killer's Draw seem to indicate that—"

"Or that's what someone wants us to think," Tower offered.

"Parker would have to be in cahoots with the Rectifiers," Bird continued. "So then, why was his wife killed? And if you think he is the P in the note we found on Downwind Dave, ordering the killing of Verhooven, why did he do that?"

Tower finished wrapping up his back and got up from the bed, stifling a groan as his ribs screamed in protest.

"I don't have the answers, Bird, but I suspect we'll find them in Big River."

Seventy-Seven

They rode into a ghost town.

Bird had never seen Big River with so few people out and about. Even the cattle yards seemed quiet.

"I'm going to the hotel to see if any of my belongings survived," Tower said. "I don't think there's much of a chance, but it's worth a look. Once I take a look, we should head over to the club. That's probably where everyone is, anyway."

"You do that, Mr. Tower," Bird said. "I'm going to go over to the saloon and see if there's any whiskey left. If there is, I'm going to restock my supply," Bird said.

They parted ways, and Bird rode directly to the saloon in the center of town. It was the first time she had ever seen the watering hole without even a single horse tied at the hitching post. She had a brief moment of panic where she wondered if there would even be a bartender on duty. That would be a disaster. Then again, she thought, it might mean that everything behind the bar was free.

She tied the Appaloosa to the hitching post while it drank deeply from the water trough. "I'm about to do the same thing, girl," Bird said. She went into the saloon and saw two old cowboys at a far table and a bartender behind the bar; other than those three patrons, the place was empty.

Bird went to the bar. "A glass of whiskey and two bottles. One open. One for the trail. The good stuff. I don't care how much it costs."

"Isn't it all good?" the bartender asked. He was a middle-aged man with a head of thinning red hair and a bright-red bulbous nose. Bird pegged him as a former drinker. Probably got too fond of his own inventory.

"That's what I always thought," she answered. "Come to find out it isn't exactly true."

The barman reached under the bar and came out with two bottles and a glass. He opened one, splashed the glass full of whiskey, and set the other bottle in front of Bird. She counted out her money, laid it down, then tossed back the whiskey with purpose.

It was smooth and smoky, and it warmed without burning. This was definitely the good stuff, she thought as she poured herself another. Her stomach wouldn't be spitting out this stuff. She wouldn't let it after paying that much.

"So, where the hell is everyone?" Bird asked the bartender, who had already turned his back on her to dry some glasses that couldn't possibly have been used recently.

He answered without turning to face her. "I heard tell there was some big meeting with the men from the club."

"Are they there?"

He set down the glass he was polishing and walked back to Bird. He shot a glance over at the old cowboys who weren't paying them any attention, then looked at her directly.

"Bartenders love to give advice," he said. "So, even though you didn't ask for any, I'm going to give you some."

"I love advice—it helps me know what not to do," Bird said.

"I know you're Bird Hitchcock and you can handle those guns of yours," he admitted, glancing down at the pistols tied down to each of her thighs. "But whatever business those men are engaged in, I would just leave them be if I were you."

"Well, you aren't me, that's for damn sure. Otherwise you'd be drinking, not serving."

"They don't care to be trifled with. Especially now. You ride out there and stick your nose in, it might be the last thing you ever do."

Bird smiled.

"You might know who I am. But you clearly don't know what I can and will do."

She grabbed the bottles.

"Now, I've got to go find that goddamned preacher."

Seventy-Eight

Tower wasn't surprised to find his room empty and his few belongings in a closet behind the hotel's front desk.

"This is all that was in there when we cleaned it out," the clerk said. She was a dour woman wearing a dark-blue dress and a tired expression. She handed Tower a bag that held some clothes.

"Policy is to clean out the room if it hasn't been paid for. Did it myself and that's all there was."

Tower could tell she wasn't telling the whole truth, but it was also clear that she looked somewhat guilty and ashamed, so he just took the bag and looked inside. Just his clothes. Everything else, including the paperwork from Martha Jeffire, was gone.

"We've all got to follow the rules, don't we?" he asked.

She shrugged her shoulders.

He left the hotel, put his belongings in his saddlebags, and rode to the saloon. Bird was just walking out with a bottle of whiskey in her hand.

"How long have you been out here?" she asked, as she untied the Appaloosa and climbed up.

"Long enough to appreciate the peace and quiet," he answered. "I don't think it's going to last very long.

They turned their horses and headed down the street toward the Big River Club.

"Find anything at the hotel?" Bird asked.

Tower shook his head. "Everything was gone. I'm guessing once those lawyer brothers surprised you and got word that you had actually left town, they went right into my room and cleaned everything out."

"I sure do hope we run into those boys," Bird said. "It's been too long since I've shot a lawyer."

"Did you find out anything at the saloon?" Tower asked. "Was there even anyone in there?"

"Unfortunately, there was, otherwise I could have just helped myself to their beverages and saved myself someone money." She glanced over at him. "You want to know what was free, though? Advice. The helpful barkeep recommended I leave the men of Big River alone while they handled whatever it is they're apparently trying to resolve."

"What did you say to that recommendation?"

"Let's just say I let him live. I don't kill a bartender unless it's absolutely necessary."

They approached the club, and the streets were still strangely absent of people. Across the way, all of the rocking chairs on the boardinghouse's porch were empty.

"This is so strange," he said to Bird. "I get the feeling everyone is hunkered down behind their doors, rifles at the ready, waiting for the bullets to start crashing through the windows."

"I tell you what, I like the town a lot more this way," Bird said. "The fewer people, the better this place is."

"That sounds antisocial," Tower said.

"As long as there are horses and whiskey, I'm fine," Bird

said. "What I don't need are a bunch of lying, sneaky, scared folks too cowardly to do what needs to be done."

They arrived at the Big River Club and again, no sign of people, horses, or activity at all.

Tower climbed off his horse, climbed the stairs, and pulled on the front door. It was locked.

"They're closed?" Bird asked. "Why am I not surprised? Probably the first time in the history of this wonderful community."

Tower looked around.

"Let's try the Cattlemen's Association."

They walked their horses over to the WCA, found another closed front door, and knocked.

Tower stepped back as the door swung inward and the face of the same woman who'd greeted Tower previously now appeared. When she saw him, and remembered his questioning of Joseph Parker, the half-smile on her face faltered.

"I'm sorry, sir, we're closed today," she said, and began to shut the door.

"Is this some kind of holiday no one told us about?" Bird, still on her horse in the street, asked. "You know, The Big River Run Away and Hide Festival?"

"I'm afraid I don't know what you mean," the woman said.

"Well, I have some information Mr. Parker would deem to be very, very important," Tower said. "Do you know where he is?"

The woman contemplated which avenue of action would bring her the least recriminations.

"Mr. Parker would be very upset if he finds out you prevented him from getting this information," Tower added. "Very upset."

The woman's decision came quickly. "He's most likely at

his ranch but I would strongly urge you not to bother him. He and some other men are having a very important meeting. They don't wish to be interrupted."

Tower turned to Bird.

"We're pretty important people, too, aren't we?"

"Of course we are," Bird said. "Hell, you talk to God all the time. How much more important can a person be?"

Seventy-Nine

They trotted their horses through the main street of Big River, on their way out of town.

"I'll be so happy when we can leave this place once and for all," Bird said.

"Agreed," Tower responded. "And I think the feeling is mutual."

On the horizon, storm clouds gathered and Tower saw a flash of lightning to the west.

He was just about to put his horse to a gallop when he heard the shout.

"Preacher!" a voice called out.

Tower turned in the saddle and saw the doctor walking quickly toward them.

"Jesus Christ," Bird said to Tower. "You just saw a doctor! My God, you are in constant need of medical attention, aren't you?"

"He's probably looking for you," Tower answered.

The doctor reached them and looked up at Tower.

"We're in a bit of a hurry, here, doc," Tower said. "Is this important?"

"I need your help," the old man said.

"Why aren't you off at Parker's ranch with the rest of them?" Bird interjected.

The doctor shook his head. "I'm not one of them. I don't get involved in their shenanigans—not that I've ever been invited. The only time I'm asked to do anything is afterward, when someone needs patching up."

"So, what can we do for you?" Tower asked. He glanced up at the sun and estimated how many hours of daylight they had left to get to Parker's ranch. The storm clouds bothered him as well. If it rained hard, it would make tracking anyone much more difficult.

"It's Frannie," the doctor said. "I don't know where she is and I'm a little bit worried about her with everything that's going on."

Tower remembered the young female assistant who had helped nurse him after the dynamite blast.

"How long has she been missing?"

"She didn't show up yesterday or today."

"Maybe she's sick or something," Bird offered.

"I don't think so," the doctor said. He looked a bit sheepish.

Tower noticed the man's expression. "What's really bothering you, doc? I'm getting real tired of everyone in this town keeping secrets."

The old man looked back toward town, then up at Tower. "It's just that, I don't know where she lives. She's a very private person."

"She didn't tell you where she lives?" Tower asked. "It never even came up in conversation?"

"It's not that she didn't tell me, it's just that she was vague. I didn't think too much of it when she told me about living north of town with some out-of-work schoolteachers. It wasn't until she didn't come in that I realized I didn't know exactly where she lived. And then I started to wonder about why I never saw these schoolteachers she said she was living with. I assumed maybe they lived closer to Harlan's Crossing or something. But it occurred to me that I never saw Frannie with anyone else."

Something began tugging at Tower's memory.

"How long has she worked for you?" Bird asked.

"She came by last spring and said she had just finished nursing school. She never said where, though, and when I asked I think she mentioned a hospital I'd never heard of. But she was nice, and very serious. No matter what condition a patient was in, missing limbs, gutshot, Frannie never flinched. The girl is fearless."

"We're heading out that way," Tower said to the doctor. "We'll do what we can."

"Thank you," he said.

Bird and Tower turned back to the trail and put heels to their horses.

"Last spring?" Bird asked.

Tower glanced over at her.

"Yes. That would have been right around the same time Bertram Egans arrived in Big River."

Eighty

"She's the one they're looking for, aren't they?" Bird asked Tower as they rode toward the Parker spread.

"It's an assumption right now," he said. "No way to prove it, but it feels right."

They didn't say anything as they climbed a rocky hill, then made their way down the other side. At the bottom, the grass was thick with standing water and mud. The horses slowed to a walk.

Bird took the opportunity to fortify herself with whiskey and share her thoughts on the missing girl.

"I've got a theory," Bird said to Tower.

"Let's hear it."

"Well, you remember that we had the idea this lady of ill repute may have come West and continued her old life, or started a new one?"

"I recall that."

"Well, what if—"

Before she could finish the thought, they climbed out of the trough of thick mud to a rise in the trail where three men on horseback waited.

Instinctively, Bird moved away from Tower before she brought the Appaloosa to a stop. More space between them made a wider target. The wider the target, the harder to hit.

She studied the three men, all of whom wore flour sacks on their heads, with holes cut out for the eyes and the mouth. To some, the sight might look sinister; to Bird, it looked ridiculous.

She and Tower stopped when they were within speaking distance.

"You know, there's no point in wearing those silly masks—everyone knows who you fools are," Bird said.

"I suggest you two turn around and go back to town," the one in the middle said. "You're about five seconds away from getting a bullet in the head."

The voice was instantly recognizable to Bird, even slightly muffled by the cloth.

"I don't think we can do that," Tower said. "We're looking for someone and since we're not wearing masks, it seems like we've got nothing to hide. In other words, we're on the right side of the law. Unlike you men."

The men on the ends both laughed.

The one in the middle said, "Actually, we are the law. If anyone is on the right side, it's us. Not you. So, let me say it one last time. Turn around, go back to town, or die out here, right now."

"Why do I have a feeling as soon as we turn around you'll shoot us in the back?" Tower asked.

"I'd say you have a problem trusting people," the one in the middle said.

"The preacher here won't say it, so I will," Bird said. "All three of you goddamned idiots can go straight to hell."

The man on Bird's right drew first. The move was so laborious and unnatural that she almost felt bad shooting him out of the saddle. The man on the far left was better with a gun, his motion was faster, but still rushed and awkward. His pistol almost cleared leather before she put two bullets into the shirt pocket over his left breast. He slid sideways out of his saddle, landed on the ground with a foot still in the stirrup, and his horse took off, dragging him behind.

The man in the middle who'd been doing the talking was so slow to react that Bird had no idea what he was going to do—neither did he, clearly.

Bird read his mind. He could turn and ride back the other way, but his job was to stop anyone going in that direction. He would have to come up with a lie about what happened, maybe claim they'd been ambushed.

Or he could ride off to either side and try to circle back to Big River, then come up with a story.

She made his decision for him.

"You've got two choices, Sheriff Chesser."

Bird saw his shoulders slump and he pulled off his sack.

"You can live or you can die," she continued. "If you want to live, drop your guns now. And since you like five seconds as a time frame, I'll give you that same amount. Do it now or die. It's that simple."

Chesser dropped his guns and held up his hands.

"Jesus, but you are a weak man, Chesser," Bird said. "You could have at least thrown some of your wooden fish at us or something. That was a pretty pathetic display for a lawman."

"Please, I just want to keep my job," the sheriff said. "I haven't done anything wrong."

"I'm sure it's quite the opposite," Tower said. "Why don't you help us out and tell us what's going on."

"I don't think I can do that," Chesser said.

"What, are you worried someone might hurt you?" Bird asked. "If that's the case, I suggest you take a good look at me and then look at your friend down there kissing the dirt."

"How many men are up at Parker's place?"

"Too many to count," Chesser said.

"And they're looking for Frannie?" Tower asked.

"Frannie? Who the hell is Frannie?"

"The girl," Tower said.

"Look, here's what—"

Before Chesser could continue, his head exploded in a cloud of pink mist. He fell off the horse to his right, indicating to Bird that the rifle shot had come from Chesser's left. She and Tower bent low and charged up the remainder of the trail, aiming for the cover of a stand of rocks, expecting more shots.

None came.

"Any guesses on who's up there and would want to shoot Chesser?" Tower asked, looking at the hill from which the rifleman most likely took his shot.

"You met the man," Bird said. "Who wouldn't want to shoot the jackass?"

Eighty-One

"I'm upset someone else shot him," Bird said. "I really wanted to."

"The question is," Tower asked, "Why him and not us? You're the biggest threat. They would have started with you, then shot Chesser, then me. And if it's Parker's men, why shoot Chesser at all?"

Bird drank some whiskey from the bottle and licked her lips.

"I think they're gone," she said.

"Maybe," Tower said. He peeked his head over the rock, saw no sign of movement, and ducked back.

Bird shoved the bottle back into her saddlebag and swung into the saddle. Both she and Tower waited for a shot, but none came.

"That wasn't one of Parker's men. It was someone else."

They rode toward the hill and circled it, but found no one and no tracks.

"I tell you, we're chasing a ghost," Bird said.

"I've had that feeling all along," Tower responded. "And I don't think we're the only ones."

They continued their course toward Joseph Parker's ranch. Bird figured they'd been on it for the last few miles.

It took them another hour of hard riding to reach the

building that constituted the heart of Parker's spread. The sun had disappeared behind a wall of thick black clouds, and a cool wind had picked up speed.

He took in the sight of the Parker ranch. The main house was impressive, as he had expected. A sprawling log home with multiple wings and gables, a wide porch that ran the width of the structure, and a host of flower beds bordering the property.

Most striking to Tower, however, was the complete absence of people, which made the ranch seem just as deserted as Big River. He had figured there would be a meeting out here and it would be busy.

The corrals were empty, the doors to all of the barns were closed. Even the cowboys' bunkhouse was deserted, the doors and windows shut and no sign of men or horses.

"They're all out looking, aren't they?" Bird asked.

"It would seem so."

Tower rode directly to the main house, climbed the porch, and knocked on the door. After several minutes without an answer, Tower knocked again.

He was about to leave when the door creaked on its hinges and an older black man dressed in a dark suit with a white shirt looked out at Tower.

"May I help you?" he asked.

"I'm looking for Mr. Parker."

"I'm sorry but he is not here."

If that was true, Tower was surprised. He hadn't figured Joseph Parker to be the kind of man who would join the hunt. Tower pictured the man seated in front of a roaring fire with a snifter of brandy in hand, waiting for word from his men that the job was done.

"Do you know where he is?" Tower asked.

"No sir, I don't."

"Do you know when he's expected to return?"

"No sir, I don't."

"What do you know?" Bird called out from behind Tower.

The black man didn't answer.

Tower thanked him, and the door was shut firmly.

He went back to his horse and looked at Bird, who sat in the saddle on her Appaloosa, a whiskey bottle resting on the pommel.

"Well, they're not in Big River. And they're not here," he said. "So, where are they?"

"They could be anywhere. This ranch is huge. Hundreds of men could get lost on this land and we'd never find them."

"Maybe we should wait here," Tower said. "Looks like a storm is moving in. I'm guessing Parker and his men are used to the comforts of shelter. They're not going to want to spend much time out there in the rain. I mean look at this place. Who wouldn't come racing back here once the weather lets loose."

"That's an option. I just wonder how much time that girl has out there alone, with every man in Big River hunting her."

Tower leaned forward, patted his horse on the neck, and looked up at the sky.

"I have an idea of what we can do."

"Let's hear it," Bird said.

"Odds are the Rectifiers are going to find her."

"I agree."

"And if they do, we both know where she's going to end up."

Bird nodded, took a last pull from the whiskey bottle, and slid it back into her saddlebag.

"Time to head to Killer's Draw," she said.

Eighty-Two

The Appaloosa realized it an instant before Bird.

Tower passed through a narrow gap between two slabs of towering rock, with Bird right behind him. Just as she reached the other side of the opening, her horse hesitated. It was the kind of movement that had no natural cause and Bird immediately reached for her gun.

For the first time in her life, however, she was too slow.

The sound of a lever-action rifle being cocked is unmistakable, and it reached Bird's ears before her pistol moved a fraction.

"Don't go for your guns, Bird," a voice said. It was a soft, feminine voice, eerily calm, almost friendly.

"Oh, don't worry about that," Bird said. She had no intention of going for her guns. As good as she was, there was no time to draw, turn, find the target above and behind her, and fire. The whole process, even for her, would take too long. She'd be dead before she turned around.

She lifted her hands away from her pistols and she couldn't help but think of Chesser doing the exact same thing not too long ago. And look how it turned out for him.

Ahead of her, Tower stopped his horse. He had heard everything and decided not to move, or even turn around. Bird appreciated his calm. Any sudden action on his part and she would be the first to die.

"That's good," the voice said. "But I need you to reach down, draw your guns, and drop them on the ground next to you. The trail is soft enough they won't fire. I know you don't like to keep an empty chamber."

Bird thought, *How the hell did she know that?* And then she did as she was told. Another first for her. This was turning out to be a day with all kinds of new things. The pistols landed on the trail next to the Appaloosa without going off.

"Now do the same thing with your rifle."

Bird complied.

"Mr. Tower, stay right there," the voice said. "Bird, walk your horse forward very slowly until you're next to the preacher, then turn around."

Again, Bird followed her instructions without fail.

She walked the Appaloosa up to Tower, then they both turned to face the trail opening and rock ledge.

"Hello, Frannie," Tower said.

The young woman who served as the doctor's assistant sat perched on the ledge, a rifle in her hands and a small smile on her face.

The Winchester in her hands did not waver, and it stayed aimed directly at Bird's chest. She also had a pistol jammed behind the belt that went around her waist.

"Frannie, don't do this," Tower said.

Bird looked closely at the girl. What she saw was an expression that had been worn by some of the most notorious gunfighters she'd ever encountered. Men who had killed so many people that they'd lost something inside. Something they knew they would never get back.

Bird would know. It was an expression she saw every time she looked in the mirror.

"I already have done it," the girl said. "I just have to finish it."

"What is your real name?" Bird asked.

"That's a great question," the girl said. "As far as I know, my mother used to call me Paige."

"Before she was murdered," Tower said. "By the Rectifiers."

The girl ignored him and held out a bundle of pegging strips, long pieces of rawhide cowboys used for all sorts of different tasks. She tossed them on the ground in front of Tower.

"The first thing I want to tell you is that I'm a crack shot and there's no way I could miss either one of you from this distance," the girl said. "The second thing is that I want you, preacher, to tie up Bird, and don't do a sloppy job of it, because I'm going to check."

Tower and Bird both dismounted from their horses. Bird tried to think of a way out of this.

"Killing them isn't going to solve anything," she said. "I'm speaking from experience. Every time you kill someone—"

"Let me guess," the girl interrupted. "Something inside you dies, too? Is that what you were going to say?"

Bird didn't respond, because that was exactly what she was going to say.

"Even if that was true, which it isn't, it's too late now." She lifted her chin toward the pegging strips in front of Tower. "Tie her up, quickly. I don't have a lot of time."

Bird turned her back and let Tower tie her hands. She sat down against a rock and Tower tied her feet. Then he turned and faced the girl.

The girl climbed down from the rocks, all while keeping her rifle on Bird and Tower. Bird noted that the plain cotton dress she'd worn at the doctor's office was now gone, replaced by denims, a dark shirt, and a leather vest. Bird could see the pockets were bulging with extra ammunition.

"You've been planning this war for some time, haven't you?" Tower asked.

The girl walked past Bird's pistols without picking them up.

"Turn around," the girl said.

Tower did so, and Bird could tell he was tempted to make his move right then and there, but he didn't. It was the right decision. Bird could tell this girl would step back, snatch out her gun, and drill Tower before he could get his hands on her.

The girl tied Tower's hands, then his feet, and nudged him toward Bird.

"Stand up, Bird," she said. Bird struggled to her feet, so much so that the girl grabbed Bird by the elbow and helped her up. Paige checked Bird's wrists, seemed satisfied with Tower's work, then guided Bird back down next to Tower.

The girl walked back to Bird's gun belt, picked it up, slung it around her waist, and tied down the guns.

"What do you know, we're the same size," the girl said. She opened the pistol's gate and spun the cylinder, making sure each was loaded.

Bird knew they were.

The girl, Paige, looked at Bird and Tower.

"Someone will be along shortly, I'm sure. But I didn't want you to interfere with me finishing this. I'll leave your horses about a mile up the trail."

"Don't—"Tower started to say, but Paige was already walking away. Bird could tell she wasn't in the mood to listen to anyone.

The girl grabbed the reins of their horses, then walked

ahead, down the trail, and Bird heard her climb into a saddle, followed by the sound of hooves pounding down the trail.

Bird leaned her head back against the rock and sighed.

"I think you liked tying me up," she said.

Eighty-Three

"Can't believe you let a youngster like her get the better of us," Bird said.

"I made it through just fine," Tower answered. "You're the one who got caught."

He struggled against the leather strips holding his wrists together. It seemed like with every effort to make them looser, they actually tightened.

"She waited for me to come through because she knew I'm tougher than you."

"She knew you were armed and that I wasn't," he countered.

"Speaking of that, how the hell do you suppose she knew so much about us? Our names? The fact that I keep all six bullets in my gun instead of five, like most?"

Tower looked down the trail in the direction the girl had gone.

"Clearly, she's wise beyond her years. I think she's been studying and planning this whole thing for a long time. She had a chance to study us because we didn't know who she was, but she knew exactly what we were doing, and why."

Tower heard Bird trying to get to her feet, but she slipped and fell back down next to him.

"We've got to get free. She's never going to survive this," Tower said. "Frannie. I should have known."

"Should have known what?" Bird asked.

"When the doctor reminded us of her name, I knew it meant something, but not until now. Francine Pascal was the name of the Baltimore prostitute in the article Jeffire had hidden."

"Frannie P.," Bird said.

"I should have realized," Tower said.

Bird struggled against her restraints. "Look, we've got time to help her. You tied me up, so you should know how to untie me," she said. They struggled to their feet, leaned against each other to gain leverage. Then they stood, back-to-back. Tower bent at his knees to lower himself so his hands were at the same level as Bird's.

She shifted her weight.

"Hold still," he said.

In the distance, they heard gunfire. One report, followed by a volley of shots.

"Hurry," Bird said.

Tower struggled, then finally managed to get his fingers on the end of one of the rawhide strips wrapped around Bird's wrists.

Holding it tight, he walked his fingers back to the knot he knew was less than an inch away. His fingers found it, and scraped at it with his thumbnail, until he was able to work the edge of his nail inside the loop. Tower felt the knot give slightly, and his thumbnail pushed through the knot. He twisted his thumb back and forth until the knot loosened.

"Try it," he said. "Go slowly, though."

Bird pulled her hands apart slowly, and Tower felt the knot loosen as she pulled and then his thumb was free.

"That's much better," Bird said. Tower turned, saw her untying the rawhide strips around her feet, then she was in front of him, working his hands free first, then his feet.

They turned and ran up the trail toward where Paige had gone. Ahead, they heard more gunfire.

"I hope we're not too late," Tower said.

Eighty-Four

The girl had been true to her word; they found the horses grazing under a stand of trees. Tower spotted Bird's rifle a stone's throw away, retrieved it, and handed it to her.

"Well, it's one more gun than I had a minute ago," she said. "Sure wish I had my pistols, though. Feel naked without them."

She checked the magazine, saw it hadn't been emptied, and then checked her saddlebags for extra cartridges. She jammed some into her pockets, then swung up into the saddle.

Tower got onto his horse, and together they took off toward the sound of gunfire.

They rode hard, Bird leading the way on the Appaloosa, which was faster than Tower's roan. She wanted to make use of what little light remained. The sun was gone, either sunk below the horizon or buried beneath the black wall of the approaching storm.

The skies were going to open up with a hellish fury at any moment. Bird dug her heels into the sides of her horse and charged ahead.

As she rode, she thought about the girl. How old had she been when her mother had come out West? Had she been there at the murder? How had she managed to find out what happened?

The trail wound its way around a hill and they splashed through a shallow stream as lightning lit up the sky and a thunderclap rattled Bird's teeth. The first huge drops began to fall.

Bird, still holding the rifle, slid it into the leather scabbard. No sense holding up a piece of metal during a lighting storm.

The Appaloosa crested a rise and shied from the trail. Bird snatched the rifle back out, knowing there was something ahead that spooked her horse. That usually meant the scent of an animal, man, or blood.

Bird was betting on blood.

They pounded down the other side of the rise, and a flash of lightning lit up the trail ahead where two bodies lay in disarray.

They were men, and Bird breathed a sigh of relief.

There were two flour sacks off to the side, and no sign of the girl.

Bird rode up to the bodies and looked down.

The men were clearly dead, their eyes wide open, pooling the fresh rainwater as it plopped down on their faces. Sections of each man's head had been blown off, but she would have recognized them anywhere.

The Conway brothers.

Tower circled around the bodies while Bird swung down from her horse and searched the bodies for guns, but found none. She bent down and rolled the first one over. All that was revealed was blood and dirt. Bird repeated the maneuver with the second brother. This time she came up with a pistol. She snapped open the cylinder and ejected two empty shells.

"I'm surprised he even got a shot off," she said. She pulled some shells from the dead man's gun belt and filled the cylinder, then snapped it into place. Bird added some more ammunition to her pocket and got back onto the Appaloosa.

"This girl is taking no prisoners," Tower said.

"I don't blame her," Bird answered.

Tower looked up at the sky, and shook his head.

"I don't either."

Eighty-Five

The darkness was painted with a flickering orange glow. Lightning split the black sky, and the rain came in waves.

"When the hell are you going to start carrying a gun?" Bird asked him.

"Same time you quit drinking whiskey," he said.

She ignored him and handed the dead lawyer's gun to him. "What's this for?"

"I can't shoot the rifle and a pistol at the same time. Makes more sense for both of us have guns than for me to have two but only able to fire one."

Tower nodded, tucking the revolver into his waistband.

They left the dead men in the middle of the trail as the rain began to lash them with a brutal intensity.

Within minutes, Bird recognized the formation ahead.

She slid her rifle from its scabbard, and waited for Tower to ride up next to her, then they both covered the short distance to Killer's Draw.

The ravine was choked with water. The rain must have started earlier, higher in the mountains, because the glorified stream now closely resembled a raging river.

Unfortunately, they were on the wrong side of it.

The scene revealed itself in yet another blast of lightning and thunder that seemed to shake the ground.

Across the river, the girl had Joseph Parker tied to the very tree against which Bird had rested after shooting Downwind Dave Axelrod. The arrogant bull Parker had always resembled was now reduced to a quivering mass of bloody wet flesh. Most of his clothes were gone, and his skin bore marks that could only have been applied by the working end of a bullwhip. His face was swollen and distorted, smeared with blood.

The girl used Parker's bulk to hide behind.

She held a pistol, one of Bird's pistols, with the muzzle firmly planted against Parker's temple.

On the other side of the river, the same side Bird and Tower now shared, were nearly a dozen men, most of them without their Rectifiers hoods, a few still wearing them. Half of the group swung their guns toward Bird and Tower, the remaining kept their aim on the girl.

Bird studied the faces of the vigilantes. She recognized a few of them, but most held no meaning for her. All of them looked scared and unsure of themselves and she understood why. The Conway brothers were dead, and their leader appeared to be moments away from the same fate.

"Get out of here, you two!" one of the men yelled. "We are in control here."

"Doesn't appear that way to me," Tower yelled back.

A thick branch, torn off from somewhere upstream, roared down the river, twisting and spinning in the wild and chaotic current.

Bird looked across the river at the girl. At her pistols. She was an expert with the rifle, but those pistols were a part of her. Extensions of her hands, really.

"Say it again!" the girl yelled. Bird could see Paige's face, wild with anger, pale as the moon with her fair hair wet and straggled, strands stuck to her ghostly translucent skin.

"We killed her," Parker said.

"Louder!" the girl yelled.

Bird saw the blood on the girl's shirt. Maybe those shots the Conway brother had gotten off found their mark.

"Who did you kill, Parker?" Paige yelled again. "Say it. I want you to say her name."

Parker thrashed against the ropes that held him in place. The girl pistol whipped him, opening up a gash along his forehead and leaving a strip of skin that hung down and flapped as he struggled.

"Francine!" he finally yelled.

"Why? Why did you kill her?"

Parker began to weep.

"I loved her!" he yelled out, his voice hysterical. "But my wife found out. She arranged it," he said. "Tried to make it look like she was a cattle thief so they could kill her," he said, looking at the group of men on the other side of the river.

Upon hearing Parker's confession, a few of the men turned and rode away.

"This is for her and my brother!" the girl yelled.

"No!" Tower yelled.

The girl pressed the muzzle into Parker's head and pulled the trigger.

Instantly, the draw erupted in gunfire with the remaining vigilantes firing across the river at the girl, and the others opening fire on Bird and Tower.

Bird had already dropped to one knee, and now she fired with a methodical precision, working the lever on the rifle so fast the shots came as a continuous roll of thunder.

Out of the corner of her eye, Bird saw the girl now using both pistols, firing with unnatural ease and speed.

The rifle's hammer clicked an empty strike plate. She was out of ammunition. She dug in her pocket for more bullets, turned to see Tower firing the pistol she had given him.

There were two men left. One of them turned to ride back to town, then fell off his horse, shot between the shoulder blades.

Bird didn't know if Tower or the girl made the shot.

She fed the last bullet into the rifle's magazine and brought it to her shoulder just as the last man standing aimed his pistol at Bird.

They fired simultaneously, and Bird heard a whistle as the bullet passed within inches of her head.

She didn't miss. Her round caught the man just under his left eye and the back of his head blew apart. He toppled over his horse and into the river, his body catching in the current and taking him away.

Men were strewn about the banks of Killer's Draw, and even with the amount of water now roaring down the wash, Bird could make out dark pools of water along the edge. Once again, she knew, Killer's Draw was running rich with blood.

Bird looked across the river and saw Tower emerging from the other side on his horse. He slid from the saddle and scooped the girl up into his arms.

Bird ran to the Appaloosa.

She hoped they could make it to Big River in time.

Eighty-Six

They arrived in Big River just as the storm was leaving. The trail had been a mess of mud and washouts but it hadn't slowed them down.

They rode directly to the doctor's office. At the sound of their horses, the door opened and the old doctor hurried out.

He took one look at them, at the girl with blood all over her, and ducked back inside.

Tower carried the girl in and Bird followed with two whiskey bottles. Tower carefully set the girl on the table where the doctor had put down clean towels and bandages. He had a stethoscope around his neck.

"Oh, Frannie," he said.

"Her name is Paige," Bird said.

"How can I help?" Tower asked.

The doctor cut away the girl's shirt and looked at the wounds. She had been shot three times. Once in the shoulder, once in the lower abdomen, and once in her upper thigh.

The doctor said to Tower without looking up, "Hold her down if it comes to that."

The old man went to a table where a row of instruments was laid out on a towel next to a pot of boiling water. He selected a scalpel and some sort of tongs.

He came back to the table and began digging through the girl's gunshot wounds. Paige opened her mouth and screamed, and the doctor used the opportunity to place a strip of wood between her teeth.

"So she doesn't bite her tongue," he said to Tower.

The doctor studied the first wound. "Passed clean through," he noted. He spent more time in the second wound until he pulled out a chunk of lead that he dropped into a pan next to the table. It landed with a thunk and Bird saw the blood dripping from it. The third wound had lead, too, but in several smaller pieces.

"She's lost a lot of blood," the doctor said. He poured some of the whiskey from one of Bird's bottles into each wound, then carefully stitched the wounds closed before covering them with bandages. The doctor then put the stethoscope on the girl's chest. "Her heartbeat is strong. I think if she doesn't get an infection, she'll live."

Tower closed his eyes, and Bird knew he was praying.

"Help me get her into this bed," the doctor said, pointing at the small room just off the main area.

Tower carried the girl to the room. Bird pulled back the blankets and when Tower placed the girl in the bed, she covered her with the blankets.

The three of them looked at each other, then left the small room and closed the door.

The doctor looked at Bird. "By my count, you've got at least one bottle of whiskey we didn't use. Let's put it to good use."

Eighty-Seven

Tower rode with Bird to the saloon, and when she went inside, he continued on. He really wanted to go back to the hotel, sleep for a month, and then leave Big River once and for all.

But something had been bothering him and he felt a strong desire to confront the issue right now. It was a night for settling scores, and this one could not be left unfinished.

Tower got to the church, left his horse by the main door, and went inside. It was silent, save for the sound of water dripping somewhere; maybe a leak in the roof had allowed rainwater to pool and it was now finding its way out. Things always managed to get where they wanted to go. Sometimes, it just took longer for them to find a way out.

He walked through the church and continued straight into the small office tucked in back.

As expected, he found Morrison sitting at the table that served as his desk, reading from the bible.

"Looking for forgiveness?" Tower asked.

He looked up at Tower, read the expression on his face. He closed the bible, and offered a weary smile.

"I was wondering if you would come back. Figured that you would."

Tower pulled out one of the chairs and dragged it well away

from Morrison. He sat so that the butt of the pistol Bird had given him was within easy reach. Morrison noted the movement.

"You're not going to need that."

"I would trust you, but I'm guessing that's exactly what Bertram Egans did and look where it got him. Facedown in Killer's Draw. Dead. Just like his mother all those years back."

Morrison shook his head. His face contorted with grief or guilt. Tower figured it was a combination of both.

"Why did you do it?" Tower asked.

Morrison looked away from Tower, at the crucifix on the wall. It was small and simple, constructed of dark pine. Handmade. Tower wondered if Morrison had made it himself.

"It was a mistake."

"It sure was. Parker and his mob didn't know about Paige. They didn't know who she was. All this time we were in town, they were trying to figure it out. They'd already killed Bertram, so who killed Parker's wife?"

Morrison nodded.

"So, I wondered," Tower continued. "If they didn't know who Paige was, then how did they find out about Bertram? That he was Francine Pascal's son?"

"It was an accident," Morrison said.

"A pretty costly accident."

"I didn't go to Parker. I went to those damned lawyers and asked a simple question," Morrison said. His eyes were watery and his nose was dripping. The words came out slow and wrenching, just like any other painful confession Tower had heard over the years. However, in this case, he was not going to offer any penance.

"It's just that right away I knew something was wrong about

Bertram. Too late, I realized what a wonderful young man he was. But by then, I had already alerted the very people who eventually . . ."

"Killed him."

"Yes, they killed him. It's just that I figured Bertram really was a preacher, but I thought there might be something else to it. Like, maybe he was going to rob the church, or banks, or fleece the congregation. So I went to those sons of bitches and asked if they could look into his background for me. You know, if they had anyone back East who could verify he was who he said he was. I honestly didn't know the history of his mother and the vigilantes!"

Morrison hung his head.

Tower remained silent.

"It wasn't until after they killed him that I started to piece it together."

Tower shook his head, allowed the anger to seep into his voice. "But why didn't you just tell me all of this from the beginning? "

"I was ashamed. And I didn't know that the girl was here, too. Bertram kept that part of the story from me. That she was his sister. I tried to hint to you that there was more to the story, but I just wanted you to go away, really. I thought maybe it was over."

"I could have helped prevent more people being killed if you told me," Tower said. "You've got just as much blood on your hands as the rest of them."

"I know," Morrison said. "Are you going to kill me?"

Tower got to his feet. He hesitated for just a moment. If Bird were here, would she kill him? It would be so easy, just take the gun out and do it.

But he knew he couldn't.

"No. But you are not going to have anything else to do with this church. I'll let Silas know what you did in exacting detail. You'll be banned permanently from the church. And if I ever see you again with a bible, or near a church, I'll personally put a bullet in your head. That's a promise."

Tower turned and left him there.

He thought he heard Morrison weeping.

Eighty-Eight

Bird, by her count, was on her tenth glass of whiskey when Tower walked into the saloon. He sat next to her at the table and she saw that he looked utterly exhausted.

"No one said doing the Lord's work was going to be easy, Mr. Tower," she said. She laughed and slugged back another whiskey. She motioned for the bartender to bring another glass.

He did so, and Bird filled it, then pushed it across the table to Tower. She filled her own glass again and raised it.

"To Paige," Bird said.

"And a full recovery," Tower added. He drank the whiskey down and pushed the empty glass toward Bird. She smiled at him. "Now we're speaking the same language," she said and filled his glass.

Despite himself, Tower laughed.

"So, where did you go?" Bird asked him.

He filled her in on his conversation with Morrison.

"I wondered about that," Bird said. "I probably would have shot him."

Tower drained his whiskey. "I know."

"Parker sure ran this town, though, didn't he?" Bird asked. "And Poor Stanley Verhooven. He must have seen the murder in progress, and knew the Rectifiers had done it, so Parker had

Downwind Dave kill him, too, just to be safe. Parker was a bloodthirsty bastard, wasn't he?"

"Some men lose their moral compass; some never had one to begin with. I suspect Parker was the latter."

"I've got a moral compass," Bird said. "And it works—I just haven't figured out how to read it."

"You're doing just fine, Bird," Tower said.

She smiled at him and glanced down at the gun still in his waistband. "You know, you look a lot more natural, a lot more comfortable, with that gun than you do with that damned bible you're always carrying around."

Tower laughed. It was a sound she could get used to. *Very* used to.

"So what now?" she asked.

"Let's check on Paige, then we'll wire Silas a short note and give him the general idea of what happened. I'll follow that up with a letter explaining the whole thing in detail. Maybe he'll want to meet so we can tell him everything in person."

Bird poured the rest of the whiskey into her glass, and drank it.

"He'll probably try to give us another assignment," she said.

She got up, went to the bar, and bought another bottle. She carried it by the neck and followed Tower out the door.

They walked down the boardwalk toward the doctor's office. Even though it was late, there were more people out than there had been during the middle of the day. Bird figured word was slowly getting out about what had happened at Killer's Draw.

The doctor was still awake. He answered the door and let them in.

"How is she, doc?" Tower asked softly.

Bird brought the bottle of whiskey to the doctor's side table and filled the three glasses that were still sitting out.

Each of them took a glass and drank.

"I just checked on her. The bleeding has stopped and her heartbeat seems stronger. She was just awake a minute ago."

"Can we talk to her?" Tower asked.

"If she's awake, but only very briefly. That girl needs to rest."

Bird followed Tower into the room.

There was a candle to the side of the bed, and the room smelled like tallow and soap.

They tried to walk softly but the floorboards creaked slightly and the girl opened her eyes.

"How are you feeling?" Tower asked.

"I survived, that's the important thing," she said, her voice barely a whisper. But she smiled, and Bird thought the girl was beautiful.

"You can rest now, it's finally done," Bird said. "You made them pay for what they did. Now, you can get on with your own life," Bird said. The words sounded so strange coming from her mouth. It sounded like advice that was usually directed at her.

"Bird Hitchcock," the girl said, her face creased with a smile.

"She needs to rest now," the doctor said from behind them.

"We're going to leave in a few days, but we'll stop by again," Tower said.

They turned to go, but the girl grabbed Bird's arm.

"The doctor said I lost a lot of blood," she said, looking at Bird, with a slight smile on her face.

"Yes, he did."

"Shhh, you've got to rest now," Tower said, motioning to Bird with his head that they needed to leave.

The girl ignored Tower and kept looking at Bird.

"Have you ever heard that expression? That blood is thicker than water?" she said.

"I have," Bird said.

"When I first saw you, I was worried you might recognize me."

Bird felt something tumble inside her. No, it couldn't be.

"What are you saying?" Bird managed to say. Her tongue suddenly felt too thick for her mouth and her brain was muddled.

The girl smiled.

"Bird, I'm your sister."

ACKNOWLEDGMENTS

I'd like to thank the entire Thomas & Mercer team for their passion and dedication to *Killer's Draw*. In particular, Jacque Ben-Zekry for her tireless efforts on my behalf. And working with the brilliant Courtney Miller has been a dream come true. In addition to being an absolute pleasure to work with, her editorial insight and prose instincts are second to none. Finally, a big thank you to Susan, Annabel, and Benna for their patience, understanding, and support during the writing of this book.

ABOUT THE AUTHOR

Dan Ames is a crime novelist and winner of the Independent Book Award for Crime Fiction. His books have reached the bestseller lists in the US and abroad. He is a member of the Mystery Writers of America and the Western Writers of America. Dan graduated from the University of Wisconsin with a degree in journalism. He currently lives with his family in Detroit, Michigan.

Kindle Serials

This book was originally released in Episodes as a Kindle Serial. Kindle Serials launched in 2012 as a new way to experience serialized books. Kindle Serials allow readers to enjoy the story as the author creates it, purchasing once and receiving all existing Episodes immediately, followed by future Episodes as they are published. To find out more about Kindle Serials and to see the current selection of Serials titles, visit www.amazon.com/kindleserials.

Made in the USA
Middletown, DE
09 September 2021

47951291R00172